A Hustler's Deceit 3

Aryanna

Lock Down Publications & Ca$h Presents
A Hustler's Deceit 3

.

Aryanna

Lock Down Publications
P.O. Box 870494
Mesquite, Tx 75187

Visit our website at **www.lockdownpublications.com**

First Edition April 2019
Printed in the United States of America
*This is a work of fiction. Names, characters, places, and
incidents either are products of the author's imagination or are
used fictitiously. Any similarity to actual events or locales or
persons, living or dead, is entirely coincidental.*

Cover design and layout by: Dynasty's Cover Me
Book interior design by: Shawn Walker
Edited by: Kiera Northington

Stay Connected with Us!

Text **LOCKDOWN** to 22828 to stay up-to-date with new releases, sneak peaks, contests and more…

Thank you!

Submission Guideline.

Submit the first three chapters of your completed manuscript to ldpsubmissions@gmail.com, subject line: Your book's title. The manuscript must be in a .doc file and sent as an attachment. Document should be in Times New Roman, double spaced and in size 12 font. Also, provide your synopsis and full contact information. If sending multiple submissions, they must each be in a separate email.

Have a story but no way to send it electronically? You can still submit to LDP/Ca$h Presents. Send in the first three chapters, written or typed, of your completed manuscript to:

LDP: Submissions Dept
Po Box 870494
Mesquite, Tx 75187

DO NOT send original manuscript. Must be a duplicate.

Provide your synopsis and a cover letter containing your full contact information.

Thanks for considering LDP and Ca$h Presents.

Dedication

This book is dedicated to my soulmate for continuing to ride with me thru it all. This love ain't mental.

Acknowledgements

Lord Jesus, I thank you for the ability to create, and the wisdom to know that I'm nothing without you. I have to thank the love of my life for the patience you breathe into me. I know that I make you want to pull your hair out at times, but as long as you know that I'm yours and you're mine, we can figure out the rest. I love you, baby! I have to thank those little ones I call my offspring for being that light in a dark world. I have to thank my family for supporting me and for sticking with me on this long winding road that is life. I have to thank my loyal fans and supporters because I appreciate the love every time you like something with my name on it. Thank you for riding with me and keeping me hungry. Special shout out to all the real men and women doing numbers that end up with a copy of my book in their hands. I hope I helped you escape the bullshit for a little while. I have to thank my LDP family for all the love and support. Let me know when you're ready for a collab. Shout out to the real Pittsburgh! I hope this one made you laugh your ass off! Tell the Buggar to act right or I'ma act up! Lol! To anyone I forgot, I apologize, but I've been up 16 hours straight and I'm cross-eyed! I love you all! Fuck the hater! Enough said.

Aryanna

Prologue

A wise man once said, "All that don't kill you can make you stronger." This is true, but *only* if you learn from it. I have a few sayings of my own to share with you. *Never test anyone!* No one is to be completely trusted. You only give them the benefit of the doubt. The amount that you give them is always weighted on what you see in their actions, and never what they say.

A man is not what he says. A man is what he does. A man's reputation is only that which people believe him to be, but a man's character is the make-up of his actions. Learn a man's character and when you have to present him with the benefit of the doubt, weigh it on what you saw and not on what he may have said, or what someone else may have told you. That is only reputation. Because no one can be one hundred percent trusted, you have to learn to tell people only what they need to know. Even God keeps secrets!

You also have to learn to keep your eyes on your friends and not so much on your enemies. Because man is half-beast, it's his nature to watch his enemy, but it's his godly-half that sleeps on those who would quickly call themselves his friend. Or maybe, even his lover. It's because of this that they are the most able to do harm, and the greatest of it. That so-called friend is so close you never see them coming, as they generally come from behind your back. Every group has a Judas!

I have no friends, just close associates, associates, and enemies. Therefore, no one surprises me. I *always* judge them by their actions or character, expecting the worse, so anything good that comes is acceptable. Remember *everyone* is a potential enemy, because everybody changes. I always leave a small space in my heart to murder even the closest person to me.

Aryanna

Chapter 1

March 2008

Zay

"Zayvion Miller, you've been charged with aggravated rape, first-degree murder, possession of a firearm by a convicted felon, use of a firearm in the commission of a felony, and felony probation violation. How do you plead?" the judge asked.

"N-not guilty," I replied, fighting not to throw up on the wooden table in front of me.

My attorney was gonna have to do the rest of the talking for me.

"Your Honor, my client isn't a flight risk and he has young children, as well as a pregnant wife, that need him home. We ask for bail to be set at a reasonable amount," Charles Swedish said.

"Uh, Your Honor, it's to my understanding that the victim of this heinous crime is the mother of Mr. Miller's newborn son, which indicates to us that Mr. Miller poses a threat, not only to the community but to his family as well," the prosecutor interjected.

It took everything in me not to leap across the aisle, pull the prosecutor's bobble head off his skinny little frame, and shit down his neck before the judge could call for order! My lawyer putting his hand on my arm was really the only thing that stopped me.

"Your Honor, the prosecution is neglecting to use the word *allegedly* with regards to the crimes Mr. Miller has been charged with. Innocent until proven guilty is still the motto of our great judicial system, therefore—"

"Save your breath, Mr. Swedish, your client won't be getting a bond. Even if I were inclined to give him one, and make no mistake I am not, his violation would prevent it. Mr. Miller, you are hereby remanded to the Virginia Department of Corrections, pending trial. Court is adjourned," the judge concluded, banging his gavel.

The sound of that hammer dropping echoed loudly in my brain, louder than it ever had before when I was in situations like this. Although, if I was honest with myself, I had to admit I'd never been in a situation quite like this one. All my life I'd been taught to expect treachery from the streets, but this knife in my back didn't come from an enemy, or even an ambitious friend. It came from my wife. It came from the one person I should've been able to trust, without doubt or hesitation and it came with a smile.

"I can file a motion for a bail hearing if you want, but we both know the judge was telling the truth," Charles said.

"No, don't worry about bond, just work on my defense," I replied.

"Hands behind your back, Miller," the bailiff ordered.

"I'll be by to see you in a day or two," Charles promised.

Once the handcuffs were secured around my wrists, I was turned towards the door that would lead me back to holding and for a moment, my eyes locked with Carmen's. She was sitting stone still in the row directly behind my seat, looking like the beautiful wife who vowed to stand by her man, but her eyes didn't hold the love required to sell that dream. Her eyes were blank and her stare was cold, but that made me smile because from this point forward, I would feel no remorse for anything I did to her. She wanted a war and she'd damn sure get one.

"I'll see you soon," I said, chuckling when her mask of indifference slipped momentarily and her lips began to quiver.

There was no need to cry now, that part would come later. I walked back into the holding tank with my head held high, because I refused to show weakness to even one mufucka in here with me. Inside though, I was all the way fucked up about the situation I was now in. Part of me wanted to mourn for Iesha because I had loved her, and for our son because he'd never know his mom the way I did. I couldn't mourn though, I could only channel my pain into anger because I was on my way back into the lion's den, and I had no idea how the fuck I was getting out this time. The only thing working in my favor was that I had an alibi in the form of the sexy doctor Dara Silver, if I could get her to testify on my behalf. I wasn't fooling myself into thinking Dara's word would be enough, because my DNA being in Jesha and my prints on the gun carried a lot of weight. I was now fighting a life sentence, and that's how I'd have to carry myself from now on.

"How long before I'm transported to Powhatan?" I asked, once I'd been put back in the holding cell and had the handcuffs removed.

"I don't know, you might spend a few days in the county jail if there's no scheduled prison runs or other people returning from court. I'll let you know," the bailiff replied, before walking away.

I was just about to ask about my bag lunch when I heard someone behind me mumbling some slick shit under his breath. I turned around slowly and evaluated the four people sharing the cell with me, trying to figure out who I was about to make an example out of.

"Only bitches whisper, so whoever got something to say needs to put some bass in their voice," I said calmly.

All eyes quickly swing to one of the three black dudes sitting on the bench to my left. On first glance, the nigga didn't look like much, just a young nigga with a bunch of tattoos. I wasn't about to underestimate his slight build or his youth though. When we locked eyes, I could tell he didn't want to repeat what he'd said, but he was smart enough to know he'd put his back to the wall.

"You ain't special, nigga, that's what I said. And I heard your charges, so—"

He never got to finish his thought before my right hook connected loudly with his right eye socket. The punch landed flush and that's what made it sound off, but his head connecting violently with the brick wall behind him was even louder. When his head bounced off the wall, I fired a left jab that took him from the bench to the floor, and I swiftly hopped on him. This was the part of the ass whooping when I was supposed to talk to him so he'd forever understand his mistake, but I was too consumed with rage to speak. As I rained punch after punch down on his quickly melting face, I was seeing Rocko and Carmen, and the hate that took over me burned hot enough to melt steel. I was only able to stop after I realized he was no longer moving. Thankfully, he was still breathing though, or I would've been fighting two murder cases.

"Anybody else got any comments, questions, or concerns?" I asked, climbing off the now unrecognizable man.

It was no surprise no one spoke a word or made eye contact. I walked slowly to the sink at the back of the cell and rinsed the blood from my hands. There was no way to conceal the cuts or the rapid swelling of my hands, but I wasn't trying to get away with what I'd done. This would serve multiple purposes, getting me transferred immediately, and also a statement. I was coming back to prison with a sex offense on my charge sheet, which meant I'd have to go ten times harder, but I didn't mind. I needed to embrace the violence and the crazy that came with it, if I wanted to keep my sanity.

"Thomas, you're up," the bailiff said, coming back through the door that led to the courtroom.

When no one moved, I assumed Thomas was the man lying on the floor, blowing blood bubbles from his swollen mouth.

"I think his lawyer might want to ask for a continuance," I said, taking his now vacant seat on the bench.

"What the fuck happened?" the bailiff asked, looking around suspiciously.

"We had a slight disagreement," I replied.

"On your feet, Miller, hands behind your back," the bailiff demanded angrily.

I took my time standing and following his instructions, which only made him all too happy to put the cuffs on extra tight.

"You're trying to add more time to whatever you're gonna get, huh?" the bailiff asked, pulling me out of the cell and pushing me down the hall to a different cell.

"Well, if I'm found guilty then it'll be a life sentence, so anything added will just be for laughs," I replied seriously.

"Yeah, well you just better hope you didn't kill him," he said, pushing me inside the cell and locking the door behind me.

14

I knew he hadn't left the cuffs on me by accident, which meant there was no point in hollering for him to come back. Instead, I took a seat on the bench and tried to organize my chaotic thoughts. It had felt good to simply let go for a little while and inflict harm but ultimately, fucking dude up didn't change the situation I was in. Aside from the obvious problem with all the charges I was facing, I was also about to come face-to-face with a mufucka I'd set up to get a life sentence. I had no doubt how that reunion would go, but deep down I knew I had to play it smart and cool.

I'd known Carmen long enough to know just how intelligent she was, but this plan that she'd set in motion took a devious intellect. I was betting that's where Rocko, her brother, came in. I didn't know the entire plan Carmen and Rocko had concocted, but I knew they hadn't gotten me sent to prison to kill me. That only left one plausible option. Leaning my head back against the cool brick wall, I ran down different advances in my mind like a rat trapped in a maze, looking for solutions to all the problems I could see. The real test though, was figuring out what to do about the problems I couldn't see. It was more than an hour before I heard the bailiff making his way towards me and he wasn't alone.

"Your ride is here, Miller," the bailiff said, opening the door for the London County deputy to enter the cell.

"Turn around," the short, stocky deputy demanded.

Again, I took my time, but the new set of cuffs put on me in place of the other ones, weren't tightened cruelly.

"He's all yours," the bailiff said, collecting his cuffs and walking away.

"I saw what you did to Thomas. If you try that with me, I'll break both your arms, making it impossible to wipe your ass or protect your ass. Are we clear?" the deputy asked.

"Yeah."

I was led out of the cell and through booking to a waiting police cruiser. Once he had me secured in the backseat, we were on the move. While a part of me was eager to get back onto familiar territory, where I could establish a routine to keep my mind occupied, a bigger part of me couldn't believe I was headed to prison again. I hadn't even made it a whole year out! The only silver lining I could find was that I'd kept shit real with my niggas on the inside, so I would be straight regardless. I would've rather been straight at home though. We made the drive to Powhatan receiving center in two hours, but I was informed I'd be put in the hole under investigation because of what happened in the holding cell. I didn't see how that was the prison's concern or jurisdiction, but the captain on duty made it clear arguing was a waste of time. So, I was taken straight to the worse place on Earth, where the heat was blistering and the roaches were bigger than midget strippers.

"Someone will be in to check your hands," the captain said, before leaving me alone.

That was good news to me because now that the adrenaline had worn off, I was feeling like my left hand might've been broken. It was another half an hour before the outer door opened again but when it did, something happened that I wasn't prepared for.

"I heard you were back, but I didn't believe it," she said.

"Yeah, I'm back. I'm surprised you're still here, Alexis."

Chapter 2

Carmen

I'd known Zayvion for more years than I could remember, and loved him for just as long. I knew everything about him, the good, the bad and the ugly, but I didn't know the man who had just been led from the courtroom. The look in his eyes and the hollow chuckle, void of humor were not normal, especially not aimed at me. When Rocko had laid out the plan to give Zay a taste of his own medicine, I knew if I actually went through with it, then Zay's love for me would vanish. It could've even turned to hate. The look he'd turned on me wasn't one of anger or hatred though, he'd simply looked at me like I was no one. Like I was a complete stranger that he'd never known or loved. I felt he'd looked at me like he wouldn't mourn my death in the slightest, and his comment 'bout seeing me soon meant he was planning to expedite my demise. Death didn't scare me. What sent chills through my body was the realization about how naïve I'd been about this entire fucked-up plan. Somehow, I'd seen a happily ever after for me and my family when the smoke cleared and the dust settled, because the man I loved most was a true street nigga who would respect my master chess move. When that gavel banged, all my childish illusions evaporated, but with that realization came the more terrifying one that there was no turning back now. I'd literally gambled with everybody's lives, so all I could do now was stack the deck, because losing was worse than death.

"Carmen, I'll do what I can to get him released, but—"

"They're not gonna let him out, but you know Zayvion like I do, so I'm sure he has a back-up plan. Your job, Mr. Swedish, is to convince him to reveal that plan so you can set it in motion, and time is of the essence," I said, rubbing my swollen stomach.

I could feel my son moving inside me, but I didn't know if it was in response to my rising agitation, or if he realized his daddy was gone. Scientific studies already theorized that a child was learning while inside the womb. And, Zay had made sure to spend time talking to his son in my stomach, so the baby would know him. So, would he now miss the sound of his father's voice? Had I really done the unthinkable and sacrificed my kid's happiness for revenge? No, not for revenge, for justice.

"Are you okay, Carmen? You look a little pale," Charles asked, taking a step towards me.

"I-I'm fine, it's just that I'd hoped to never be in this situation again, but here we are."

"I have to be honest with you, this is the last thing I saw Zayvion doing, and even with the evidence they have against him, I'm not convinced," Charles said.

"What do you mean?" I asked nervously.

"I mean, Zayvion is a lot of things, but messy isn't one of them. You really think he was smart enough to know your brother's prints on a gun would seal his fate, but he'd be dumb enough to leave his own prints on a murder weapon and DNA evidence?" Charles asked rhetorically.

"Maybe it was a crime of passion or—"

"Or a set-up," Charles interjected, looking around to see if anyone was paying attention to our conversation. I wasn't liking this lawyer's train of thought, but I had to appear to be the concerned wife in order to learn more.

"Set-up? Is that what Zay told you?" I asked.

"We didn't really discuss anything when I saw him at the jail yesterday, other than my retainer and today's arraignment," Charles replied.

"Well, I know his defense is gonna cost a lot, but with the baby coming, I don't know when I'll be able to pay—"

"You don't have to worry about that Carmen, it's all taken care of," Charles said, quickly.

"It-it is?" I asked, surprised.

"Yeah, I thought Zayvion told you all of this when he got out the last time. He made sure to take the necessary precautions, just in case he ended up in this type of situation again," Charles replied, unable to hide the confusion on his face, undoubtedly a byproduct of the bewilderment on my face. I shouldn't have been surprised that Zay was thinking several steps ahead, but I was getting a bad feeling about all of this.

"Zay didn't mention to me any steps he took, but he probably just forgot because he had so much going on. If you have time, maybe we could—"

"Mr. Swedish, I need to speak with you about your client," the bailiff said, suddenly appearing at Charles's side.

"Of course. Carmen, I'll call you as soon as I can and we'll get together," Charles promised, quickly gathering his briefcase and disappearing with the bailiff.

There was no doubt in my mind the client referred to was Zayvion, but I had no clue as to what could be so important all of a sudden. What I did know was that if they somehow let that nigga out right now, I was as good as dead and no amount of police would save me. Knowing that, I grabbed my purse and waddled my big ass out of the courtroom. As soon as I got to my car, I pulled my phone out and sent a text message to my new best friend, letting her know what was going on. A sharp pain in my stomach had me on the phone with the quickness, scheduling an immediate appointment with my doctor, while trying to fight off the panic I was feeling. What I'd done, I'd done for my brother but if this shit didn't go right, my brother wouldn't be able to protect me. The taste of regret was heavy on my tongue, because Zay was the wrong nigga to cross, but he'd left me no choice.

I started my 2009 Denali and pointed it in the direction of my doctor's office, praying nothing was wrong with my son. He was only a couple weeks from his expected arrival into this world, but I knew anything could still happen between now and then, and I wasn't taking no chances with his health. I could hate his daddy all I wanted to, but my babies were innocent in all of this shit. As I drove, I tried to figure out what I was gonna tell Ariel and RJ about Zayvion not being around. Even though RJ knew Rocko was his father, he'd still gotten used to Uncle Zay being around when he needed him. And, no matter how old Ariel got she'd always be a daddy's girl, which would make her separation from Zay just as hard as the last time. Xavier wasn't even a month old yet, so he wouldn't be affected yet by Zay's incarceration, but he was already showing clear signs of missing his mother. Torturing her by shoving Zay's pistol in her stanking ass pussy, and then putting two bullets in her head, had brought me great satisfaction. It was temporary though, and now when I listened to that newborn cry for his mother, I felt something like guilt. The guilt wasn't because I'd killed her trifling, home wrecking, nothing ass bitch, but because Xavier had been affected. He was just as innocent as his siblings and to cancel out my guilt, I would raise Xavier as my own. Thankfully, what little family Iesha had hadn't put up a fight about that, but I'd suspected as much because they knew they couldn't love a baby whose father had taken what they'd loved most. It took more than strength to do that. I made it to my doctor's office within forty-five minutes, and was quickly ushered into the exam room once I came through the front door.

"I wasn't expecting to see you for a couple weeks, Carmen," Dr. Dara Silver said, following me into the room and closing the door behind us.

"I know, but I-I need you to check him and make sure he's alright," I replied, scooting up on the exam table and pulling my t-shirt up over my stomach.

"Don't you wanna wait for Zayvion, because—"

"Zayvion ain't coming," I said.

"Of course he will, especially if you called him so—"

"Zay's not coming!" I shrieked, fighting against the tears that wanted to run freely down my face.

There were so many emotions coursing through my body, I thought I was gonna pass out, but then the doctor took my hand and began coaching me through breathing exercises. Slowly, my heart rate returned to normal and the darkness that had been encroaching on my field of vision pushed back some.

"Th-thank you," I mumbled, slightly embarrassed by my outburst.

"It's okay, sweetie, now let's take a look at your little passenger," she replied, setting up the ultrasound machine.

Once she had my stomach coated with the necessary jelly, she turned the machine on and instantly, it sounded like a whirlpool in surround sound.

"His heartbeat is strong and there he is," Dara said, pointing at the screen.

My sigh of relief was louder than my son's heartbeat and despite my best efforts, the tears I'd been fighting slid from my eyes.

"Everything is fine, Carmen, but I still think that you should let me call Zay for you so he can—"

"He can't and he won't come. He's locked up," I said softly.

"Locked up! What the fuck for?" she asked, excitedly.

The change in her demeanor caught me off guard, but I had no doubt it was shocking to hear what I'd said. Dara Silver may have had the big ghetto booty of a black girl, with the rest of the body to match, but I doubted she spent time with mufuckas like Zayvion.

"It's a long story, but more than likely, Zay won't be around for a while," I replied.

"Wow, Carmen. I mean, I'm not judging or anything, but I find it crazy that he would put himself in a fucked-up situation when he has kids to take care of."

"Yeah, me too. I just came from his arraignment and the stress of it all is how I ended up laid up on your table," I said, once again looking at the screen with my baby's image and heartbeat on it.

"Arraignment? Oh, so this just happened."

"Yeah, he got arrested yesterday," I replied, using the paper towels she handed me to wipe my stomach off.

"Did they at least give him a bond or does he have to sit in the county?" Dara asked.

"No, no bond. New charges mean an automatic probation violation and he's sent back to prison immediately, but they wouldn't have given him a bond on a murder charge anyway."

"M-murder?" she stammered, pausing in her movements to look squarely at me.

I hadn't meant to say as much as I had, but the shit would be on the nightly news regardless.

"Yeah, murder. He'd gotten some other bitch pregnant and he killed her. Maybe because she had the baby a couple weeks ago, or maybe because she didn't want to be with him anymore. All I know is that he raped her and killed her, and now I'm stuck raising his side chick's baby," I said, frustrated.

"W-when?" Dara whispered.

"Two or three days ago."

"Impossible," she replied, in a suddenly stronger voice.

"What? What do you mean? I know what the police said when I went to see him at the jail, and they said it couldn't have been more than two or three days," I replied, becoming more annoyed.

"I-I was just saying it's impossible for all this to be happening to you, especially right now."

Our eyes locked for a moment, but then she went back to putting her equipment in its proper place and I fixed my clothes.

"I appreciate you taking the time out to see me on such short notice, Dara, and I'm sorry for all the craziness I brought with me," I said, climbing down off the table.

"It's okay and it's understandable. I told Zay he shouldn't be causing you undue stress this close to your due date."

"You did? When was this?" I asked, searching my memory to recall my last doctor's visit.

"It-it was during your last checkup I think, or maybe the one before that. The important thing is that you go home, get some rest, and think positive because I'm sure Zayvion will be home soon," she replied, smiling.

I knew her comments were meant to be soothing, but the conviction with which she spoke about Zay coming home only made me more anxious.

"Whatever you say, Dara," I said, walking slowly towards the door.

When I pulled it open, I had every intention of walking through and getting on with the rest of my day, but I was suddenly frozen in place.

"Uh, Doc, I think we have a problem," I said slowly.

"What's that?"

"Well, you're a sexy female, but I don't think all this wetness I'm feeling between my legs is because of you," I replied, turning around to face her.

"Oh," she said, looking down at my newly soaked jeans.

"Tell me this ain't happening," I moaned, suddenly feeling pressure in my lower stomach that equaled a soccer kick.

"Don't panic, just move back to the table," Dara replied, moving swiftly to my side and guiding me back to where I'd come from.

As soon as my back hit the cushioned table a contraction rocked me, snatched the breath from my lungs, and rendered me speechless until it passed.

"Ho-ly-shit!" I exclaimed, once I stopped seeing double.

"Just breathe, you've done this before," Dara coached, holding my hand and breathing with me.

"I-I'm breathing, but-ugh-shit!" I screamed in pain.

"Yeah, it's definitely happening. You're having this baby."

Aryanna

Chapter 3

Rocko

"Vargas, you're wanted in medical!" C.O. Hardy yelled from the gate.

"Kayla, play my hand," I said, passing my cards to my cell as I stood up.

"He gambling with your money?" White Mike asked.

"Yeah, he good," I replied, making my way to my cell to change my shoes.

It was a friendly spade game, but a few dollars could ruin a friendship quick in prison, so the best thing in the world was an understanding. Truthfully, I wasn't worried about the two dollars a game I'd just been playing for, because I was more interested in the unexpected trip to medical I was about to make. I knew Abby was working, but our rendezvous wasn't supposed to be until tonight after pill call. Her switching up the game plan without warning was unusual, but I tried not to let my mind go to the worst-case scenario of something being wrong. With her being four months pregnant, she'd made it through a lot of the first trimester's dangers, but it was still possible for her to miscarry. That would devastate both of us, and just the thought of losing my daughter quickened my steps after I had my sneakers on.

"You got my pass?" I asked C.O. Hardy as I approached the gate.

He passed the piece of paper to me and popped the gate without any smart-ass remark, which I was thankful for. I quickly made my way downstairs to medical, where I found Abby standing outside in the hallway waiting on me. That wasn't normal either.

"Give me your pass," she demanded, before I could speak.

I handed it to her and watched while she passed it to the C.O. sitting just inside the doorway. I didn't hear the words they exchanged, but when she turned back to face me, she signaled for me to follow her around the corner.

"Medical is full right now, so I'll be checking your vitals in the eye doctor's office," she informed me.

Her tone was casual and probably sounded normal to anyone around us who might have been listening, but I could hear the anxiety in her voice. Something was definitely up. I didn't say shit though. I simply followed her lead down the hall and into an office.

"What's wrong?" I asked, as soon as the door was closed behind us.

"He's here!" she whispered fiercely.

I didn't have to ask who "he" was, but I was definitely surprised by how fast Zayvion had been transferred to prison.

"Already? Where is he?"

"In the hole across from medical, but he's being examined and I didn't know if he was gonna have to be brought into medical, so that's why I brought you over here," she replied.

"Examined? Wait, why would they put him straight in the hole?" I asked, confused.

"Because he beat somebody half to death when they had him in court's holding area. I'm not sure exactly what happened, all I know is I got a text from your sister, telling me he was locked up with no bond, and I figured he'd be here in a few days. The next thing I know, we're notified he's on his way in and needs to be looked at, because he was in a fight. Naturally, I wanted to know the details of the situation and it wasn't a fight, Zayvion beat a man. He beat him, Rocko! And, you think you're gonna be able to reason with this psycho?" she asked.

Her asking me this put her anxiety into perspective, and helped me to understand why she'd called me down here. She was about to panic.

"Baby, I can tell you're worried and that's not good for our little girl," I said, putting my hands on her stomach and kissing her on the forehead.

"But, Rocko, he's dangerous and—"

"I know who Zayvion is and what he is, and I'm telling you I can handle him. You're just gonna have to trust me and stick to the plan," I said, calmly.

"The-the plan? You actually want me to go have a conversation with this crazy motherfucker?"

"Not without there being a locked door between you two, but ultimately yeah, I want you to go to him and explain that we need to work together to get out of here. Or, he'll never see his kids again," I replied.

I could see the skepticism on Abby's face, but I knew how Zay would react to my ultimatum. By now, Zay understood that he'd lost Carmen and why he'd lost her, but he was smart enough to see it could get worse for him. Carmen could simply disappear, and he'd be left forever wondering what became of his kids, while he rotted away in prison for a crime he didn't commit. Honestly, it would be poetic justice, but I wanted freedom more than I wanted that. I no longer had the connections to make a break out and clean getaway possible, but Zayvion was more powerful than ever. All he needed was a little convincing to do the right thing, and maybe a peace offering.

"When you go see him, I want you to give him this," I said, moving to the desk behind her and jotting down a quick note.

I watched her read it, then look at me and then read it again.

"Why are you getting involved in this?" she asked.

"Because it shows I'm okay with co-existing with this nigga as long as we're working towards the same goal. I need him alive, so that means whether I like it or not, I've gotta be that extra set of eyes and ears he needs in here. And, I need your help to do that," I replied, pulling her into my arms and kissing her soft lips.

I could feel her trying to resist the spell I intended to weave with my mouth, but we both knew it was useless.

"W-we don't have long," she said, already breathing heavily while unzipping my jumpsuit.

"It won't take long," I replied seductively, pushing her backwards until her ass bumped into the desk.

With hurried motions, I pulled her scrubs and panties down, allowing her to pull one leg free so she could open her legs to take what I had to give. Our bodies molded together like hand in glove as I pushed through the gates of her heaven, submerging myself in her heat. She was incredibly tight and wet, making it difficult for me to try and fuck her fast, but time was of the essence and I needed her in the worst way. I played it cool for the first couple of strokes, but the moment she locked her legs around my waist and her arms around my neck, the savage in me came out.

"Rocko, Rocko! I—"

"Shhh," I whispered, before clamping my mouth down on hers to catch her sounds of passion.

The last thing either of us needed was for someone to hear what we were doing. Even knowing that didn't stop me from diving inside her with greed on my breath and lust in my eyes, but I did pick her up off the desk and carry her to the back corner of the room. With her back literally up against the wall, I fed her dick in steady strokes, loving how her pussy took the punishment and begged for more. Within minutes, she was cumming and struggling not to scream, as wave after wave of her orgasm crashed over her. Normally, I would've insisted on multiple orgasms before letting go, but instead I rode the tide of her climax to my own fulfillment. I held her up against the wall until my dick stopped throbbing inside her and her body stopped trembling, but even after I let her down, I could still feel her tightness all around me.

"H-have I ever told you that your pussy is amazing?" I asked, fighting to catch my breath.

"You might've mentioned it before," she replied, laughing.

"I'll say it again, baby, amazing! Will I see you again tonight?"

"I don't know, that depends on when you want me to handle this situation," she replied, fixing her clothes.

I could tell she still wasn't happy about dealing with Zayvion, but I knew she'd do what was necessary, because it benefited her in the long run.

"To be real with you, it needs to be taken care of ASAP, but I don't understand why that would prevent us from getting together," I said.

"Because I won't go see him until nighttime pill call. I'll have to switch out with the nurse who normally does the medication for people in the hole."

"Will it draw suspicion if you ask to do her job?" I asked.

"No. She knows I'm pregnant, so I'll just tell her I'm not feeling good and I don't feel like dealing with a bunch of inmates tonight."

I contemplated what she'd said while fixing my own clothes, but I was studying her the whole time, wondering if I was causing her too much stress.

"Baby, you know I appreciate everything you do for me, but maybe it's time we revisited the conversation about you working here," I said.

"There's nothing to revisit, Raymond, I told you I'm riding with you for better or for worse. I don't want to argue about that again."

The fact that she was using my first name told me she was more than ready for a fight though, and that was the last thing I wanted. While she busied herself with straightening up the room so it looked normal, I picked up the note up from the floor that she was gonna deliver to Zayvion. I knew he wouldn't take my warning at face value, but he was still plugged in enough to verify what I was putting him up on.

"Remember, I don't want you meeting with this nigga without there being a door between you two. I don't think he'll hurt you, but that's not a chance I'm comfortable with taking at this point," I said, passing her the piece of paper again.

"I understand, and you already know I'm gonna do what you say."

I pulled her into my arms and kissed her thoroughly enough to have both of our hearts beating fast, but she stopped me before we got past the point of no return.

"I'll miss you tonight," I said genuinely.

"I'll miss you too, but you'll be home soon."

"You sound sure of that, almost like you know something that I don't," I replied, looking at her closely.

"I just believe in you and your sister, and I don't think she would've gone along with the plan if she wasn't sure it would work. You're not spending the rest of your life in here. You're coming home to me and our kids."

"I definitely like the sound of that," I said, smiling and kissing her one more time.

"I gotta get you back, but your ass still better call me tonight," she stated, looking at me with a serious expression on her face.

"Don't I always call your crazy ass? Plus, if I don't, I know you'll be blowing my cell phone up and that's a bad look. I got you, baby, I'll call you by ten p.m., I promise."

"Okay, come on," she said, kissing me quick before sticking the note I'd given her in her bra and opening the door.

I strolled casually out of the room like nothing was out of the ordinary, and I didn't smell like good pussy. After picking my pass up from the C.O.'s desk at medical, I made my way back upstairs, resisting the temptation to pause by the hole and say something smart to Zay. The time would come for me to gloat but for now, I'd have to celebrate my first round of victory inwardly.

"What the fuck are you smiling about?" C.O. Hardy asked when I got back upstairs.

"The DNA results just came in and I'm not the father of your wife's baby, so she can leave me the fuck alone now!" I replied, handing him my pass.

The look on his face only made me smile wider, even though I knew I'd end up paying for it later. It was worth it now though. Hardy was still speechless when he opened the gate to let me back onto the pod floor, and that made me laugh as I walked away. On my way to my cell, I signaled for my dude Farmer to follow me, because I felt like partying a little.

"I want you to bring me about a quarter of an ounce out of the weed you're holding for me because I'm trying to get faded," I said, once we'd gotten to my cell.

He turned and left without a word, returning five minutes later with that good loud that was sure to have me cross eyes real soon. Ordinarily, I wouldn't smoke with Hardy working, but his shift would be over in less than an hour, and that meant his focus was on waddling out the front gate. After I gave Farmer something for him to smoke, he left and I called Kayo to the cell.

"You trying to blow a couple?" I asked.

"You already know I'm with it," he replied, closing the door and putting the towel under it to keep the smell from escaping.

While I rolled a few blunts, Kayo put oil on the lamp and covered the window, so by the time I sparked the spliff we were in our own cocoon.

"Everything good?" he asked, once I passed him the blunt.

"Yeah, everything is straight. I just got some good news, so I wanted to celebrate a little!"

Kayo knew about Abby, but he didn't know about the play I had going when it came to Zayvion. That had to stay completely under wraps, because I couldn't afford for anything to go wrong or get in the way.

"I'm down for a celebration any day if it allows me to escape this bullshit. You know we're gonna have to find somebody to cook for us though, because after one blunt your ass is gonna be past the moon," he said, laughing.

"Don't act like you ain't a lightweight, my nigga, because you be deep in space with me!" I replied, lighting another blunt.

We ended up smoking a total of four blunts, which resulted in us being stuck in our cell until they came around and locked the door before last count. I was laying down, waiting on count to clear so I could pull my cell phone out and call Abby, when suddenly my door was unlocked and pulled open.

"Which one of you is Vargas?" a tall sergeant asked, stepping in the cell.

"That's me, why?" I asked sitting up.

"Pack up, you're getting transferred," the sergeant replied, tossing me a few black trash bags.

My first thought was that the bitch mufucka Hardy wrote me up and lied on the paperwork, but then I realized that the sergeant said transferred and not that I was going to the hole.

"Transferred where?" I asked, still not moving to pack.

"To another prison, now hurry up. Your ride's waiting."

Chapter 4

Zay

"Why are you surprised that I'm still here?" Alexis asked curiously.

"Because the last time I saw you, your boss was whooping your ass, and that would kinda make it hard to work with each other. Or not," I replied, looking at her with disdain.

I could admit that when she and I had started fucking around during my last stint at this particular spot, I hadn't started out with plans of forever. Still, I'd caught feelings, genuine feelings, so it still stung that she played me by fucking with someone else, without even casually mentioning it to me. I would've respected her more if she would've kept it real and said it was complicated, instead of telling me she was single.

"First of all, he wasn't my boss because I'm a contract employee, not a state employee. More importantly though, having a domestic violence charge didn't look good to his supervisors, so he was told to seek employment elsewhere," she replied.

"Do you need his cell opened?" a C.O. asked from somewhere beyond my vision.

For a minute, she simply stared at me and I couldn't tell exactly what she was thinking. Maybe she was wondering if I was gonna beat her ass like her ex had. I couldn't say she didn't deserve it, but that wasn't how I got down.

"Yeah, I do need his door open so I can thoroughly examine him. I'd take him over to medical, but it's a mad house in there," she replied.

Within seconds, a tall and slim white C.O. stepped in, unlocked my cell and disappeared just as quickly. When she pulled the door open, I didn't immediately take a step back but instead, I stood there and looked her over from head to toe. There wasn't lust in my eyes nor in my heart, I just wanted her to feel the power of my stare.

"Are you done?" she asked, smirking.

My answer was to back up slowly until my knees met my bunk, and I took a seat.

"Let me see your hands," she instructed, turning on the light as she came towards me.

"You wanna check my hands first? What if I have a broken rib or something?"

"I already saw photos of the other guy and with the way he looked, it's clear he didn't land a punch. He's still alive though, in case you were wondering," she replied, sitting her bag containing her medical supplies down, and reaching for my hands.

I could tell by the expression on her face, she felt something when she touched me and that made me smirk.

"Nah, I wasn't wondering if he was still alive, I couldn't care less," I said honestly.

"Yeah, I thought that might be the case when I heard why you were back. How did you end up in a trick sack, Zayvion?"

"What makes you so sure that it was some trickery involved?" I countered.

"Because I know you, and I know you wouldn't do no shit like that. Especially not to Jesha, because I know you had genuine love for her."

"You're full of shit, Alexis, because if you thought I had love for her, you wouldn't have been fucking me."

"Wouldn't I? I said you had love for her, I never said I did," she replied quickly.

"Ah, so as long as you got what you wanted, it didn't matter. Well, at least now you're being honest."

"I didn't necessarily get what I wanted though, did I?" she asked, looking me directly in the eyes even as she continued to check my hands.

"Sure you did. You got money, dick, and you got to sell a dream so—"

"I didn't get you though, and that's what I really wanted. I know that that's my own fault, but don't try to minimize what we had because it was special," she said.

"You can tell yourself all the lies you need to, Alexis, but don't bullshit me because I know that I'm not what you really wanted. You wanted to have your cake and eat it too, but you fucked up by not keeping shit real," I said, pulling my hands away from her.

"Zayvion, I swear it wasn't like that, and I don't have enough time to explain right now, but on the lives of my children, I promise my love for you was real. It still is."

A big part of me started to call her promise bullshit, no matter who she swore on, but the look in her blue/green eyes was genuine. If I was being real with myself, I'd have to admit I wouldn't still be this mad at her if my feelings for her weren't real. And we both knew that I lived in a glass house, which meant I was the last mufucka who should be throwing stones.

"Saying you still love me doesn't change what happened," I replied.

"You're right, it doesn't, but it's true. I love you, and I'm so sorry for how the skit ended between us. I'm not even asking for your forgiveness right now, I'm just asking that you let me make it right."

"And how are you gonna do that?" I asked.

"First things first," she replied, backing up out of my cell.

"C.O., can you go down to the kitchen and get a bag of ice for Mr. Miller's hands, because they're swelling steadily? I can continue his examination if you'll just handcuff him."

It was on the tip of my tongue to ask this bitch if she'd lost her mind, but she leveled a look at me that demanded silence before I could open my mouth. The C.O. quickly reappeared, instructed me to turn around, and put cuffs on me.

"You sure you'll be okay with him for a few minutes?" the C.O. asked.

"I'll be fine," Alexis replied, flashing a disarming smile.

The C.O. stepped out of the cell, but neither of us moved until we heard the outer door shut.

"We don't have much time, so you're gonna have to multi-task," she said, closing the distance between us and swiftly pulling my dick free from my pants.

"Mul-multi-task how?" I asked, watching in amazement as she quickly dropped to her knees.

"Answer my question, who put you in the trick sack?"

My immediate response was a low moan, because she'd popped my dick in her mouth and was sucking it like there was bubble gum at the center. The torture of having my hands restricted was real, but I could control my hips just fine.

"Zay, stop trying to fuck my face and answer me," she said, popping my dick right back between her lips.

"It-it was C-Carmen and her brother," I stammered.

Thankfully, she didn't stop once she heard my answer, but she did hum thoughtfully, which only added pleasure to the situation. I knew it would be a mistake to look down at her, but I did it anyway, and I was immediately transfixed. The way her eyes blazed up at me as she made every inch of my dick disappear down her throat, had warning bells creaming in my brain. Of course I ignored them and kept watching, trying to decide if I was more turned on by what she was doing to me, or the pleasure she was taking from it. In the end it didn't matter though, because it led to the same result.

"A-Alexis! I'm about to c-cum," I warned.

"Mmm-hmm," she replied, increasing her speed.

In the distance, I could hear footsteps and keys approaching, but my senses were quickly scrambled as I came hard enough to turn my knees to jelly. When the key went into the lock for the outer door, Alexis was still slurping the last of my life out of me, but by the time the lock turned, she had my dick tucked away and she was on her feet.

"Perfect timing," she said, turning to the C.O. and taking the bag of ice from him. I wanted to collapse onto my bed, but I had to remain standing while the cuffs were remanded.

"I'll only be a couple more minutes," she said.

"I'll be right outside," the C.O. replied.

"That was crazy," I whispered, shaking my head.

"You think so? Wait until I get you alone. Let's talk business though, because I could've sworn you said that your wife and her brother got you into this mess."

"That's exactly what I said," I replied, feeling the rage Carmen's betrayal inspired rush to the surface.

"Wow. Okay, so tell me that you have a plan."

My silence was all the answer she needed, because now she was shaking her head.

"Looks like we're gonna have to figure this one out together then, and don't give me that look, because I'm here for *whatever* you need," she vowed.

I'm smart enough to know that in my current situation beggars can't be choosers, so I didn't say any of the smart shit I was thinking. If this bitch thought I was gonna trust her because she had my dick and cum on her breath, then she was more foolish than I ever thought.

"You know what I need first," I replied.

"Yep, and I'll have it by tomorrow. Oh, and just to be clear, I'm not dealing with anyone on any level. I don't care if you are because I know I have to earn my spot back, but make no mistake I will earn my spot back," she said.

When I nodded my head, she passed me the bag of ice and began to gather her medical supplies together. After making sure she had everything, she kissed me quick on the lips while squeezing my dick, and then walked out of the cell while making sure to swing her juicy ass enticingly. I honestly hadn't thought that I missed her, until now. I could argue with myself that I just missed the sexually chemistry, but that would be me trying to ignore all that we'd had once upon a time. As much as I'd loved Carmen, I had still been planning to run away with Alexis, so it had been more than sex. What it would be now was what I didn't know, but that wasn't even my main question or concern. My focus had to be on Carmen. Despite my hands starting to ache, I sat the bag of ice in my sink and I laid down on the thin-ass mattress the state considered a bed. The pain and discomfort I felt was soothing in a way that chewing gum is for someone who use to smoke. It wouldn't be enough though. I didn't know if I had more love or hate for Carmen, but either way she had to answer for what she'd done. Was I guilty of betraying her by getting another bitch pregnant? Absolutely! But, that action didn't cost her her life, unlike what she intended to happen to me. It was okay though because as the old saying goes, the road to hell is paved with good intentions. Carmen would find that out firsthand, just as soon as I figured out how to get out. I told myself I was closing my eyes to better visualize my plans for my treacherous wife, but before I knew it I was sucked into the land of unconsciousness, dreaming about Jesha. At first my dream started off pleasant, with us fucking like animals in the middle of a field but suddenly, Carmen was looking over us with my gun in her hands. The sound of thunder following her dropping the hammer snatched me out of my sleep, forcing me to sit straight up in bed. Even being as disoriented as I was, I still felt her presence before I heard her gasp.

"Who are you?" I asked, looking at the slender built brunette standing outside my cell door. When she glanced to her right at the C.O., I could see the fear in her eyes, but I didn't understand it.

"M-Mr. Miller, it's time for your Ibuprofen," she mumbled.

I watched her closely as I got up, noticing how she took an involuntary step backwards as I neared her. Right then I doubted Alexis had sent her to me, because she was way too shaken for that, so maybe she'd heard about my charges or something.

"What's your name?" I asked.

"W-why?" she countered, somewhat panicked.

"Because I thought you might take it disrespectfully if I simply called you nurse, and I don't want to disrespect you."

"Oh, my name is Abby," she replied, sheepishly.

"Okay, well thank you for bringing my medication, Abby," I said, holding my hand out.

This time when she looked to her right, it wasn't a fear induced movement. I could tell she was on some sneaky shit. Sure enough, her hand shot out and dropped a kite on my floor right before she put the ibuprofen in my palm. By the time I'd bent down to retrieve the note, I heard the outer door shutting, and I looked up to find nothing except air where she used to be. Had it not been for the things I was holding, I would've sworn that Abby had been no more than a figment of my imagination. After taking the Ibuprofen with a chaser of nasty sink water, I sat back on my bed preparing to read my mystery note. Instantly, my anger was back and I understood why sweet Abby had been so scared of me. I took several deep breaths and pushed my anger down enough to read the note in its entirety.

Welcome back, old friend! I would say I could imagine how you feel, but I don't have to because I'm living the same nightmare you are. Bet you didn't see this coming, huh? You thought fast talk and good dick would break the bond Carmen and I share? You should've known better! Being that you're back in prison, you now know she never believed your lies, but she is willing to forgive you if you get me out of here. The choice is very simple, because I'm sure you're figured out by now if you don't get me out, Carmen is gonna take everything you own, pack up the kids and disappear far from your reach. You've got the resources to make all of this go away for both of us, so I suggest that you do just that. And to show you there's no hard feelings between us while we're stuck in this situation, I'm gonna put you up on game real quick. Your cousin, Hem, is asking questions about your sudden departure coinciding with my sudden arrival. He's asking the wrong kinds of questions, you feel me? I would suggest you handle that ASAP before it handles you. There's plenty of grass, but you gotta remember you're not the only snake.

Aryanna

Chapter 5

Carmen

"No, no I'm not gonna push, because it's not fucking time to push! My son is not done yet!" I yelled frantically.

"It don't matter if he's done, sweetie, he's coming. Your water broke and you're ten centimeters dilated, so push," Dara instructed from in between my spread legs.

When my water had broken and she confirmed I was in labor, I'd argued that I couldn't have the baby unless I was in the hospital. She'd shot that down because she was my doctor, her office was staffed and equipped, and there was no time to move me. I'd argued for drugs, lots and lots of drugs, but she was quick to remind me I'd often said I wanted a natural birth. Right now, I wanted to give this bitch a natural ass whooping! Part of me wanted this ordeal called labor to be over with, but my heart was breaking because Zayvion wasn't here, and that was my fault. He'd been right by my side, holding my hand and coaching me when Ariel was born. Despite the pain I'd been in, I'd loved him more than ever before, because he'd been there for every contraction until our little girl was there for us to hold. That wouldn't happen this time though, this time I was on my own and it was my own damn fault. Truthfully, I was more worried that Zay couldn't forgive me for this as opposed to everything else I'd done.

"Come on, Carmen, push," Dara encouraged.

With tears streaming down my face I did like I was told, finally accepting that no matter how much I prayed, I couldn't turn back the hands of time. A short five minutes later, my son screamed his way into the world in rockstar fashion. I was happy he was perfect and healthy, but I was emotionally drained by everything else. Seeing Dara cut the umbilical cord instead of Zayvion had me wanting to openly sob, but I kept it together as I waited for her to clean and wrap my son. There would be time to shed tears for the sorrow I was feeling, but now wasn't that time.

"Here he is, Carmen, your six-pound, five-ounce bundle of joy," Dara said, gently handing him to me.

My little man was already yawning, like he'd just worked the hardest day of his life, but he still looked gorgeous. And, he definitely looked like his father. For every second I stared at him, the question of how I could hate his father enough to do what I did grew louder in my mind, until it was screaming at me. Did Zayvion fuck up? Yes! Did he deserve to spend the rest of his life rotting in prison away from his kids? God help me, but I couldn't say that with the same conviction I'd once felt.

"What are you gonna name him?" Dara asked, intruding on my thoughts.

"Name him? Isn't it obvious, since he looks just like his damn daddy?" I replied in a bitchy tone.

I could tell by the expression on Dara's face that the way I'd come at her had caught her by surprise, which made two of us.

"I'm sorry, Dara. Not having Zay here for this moment is weighing on me," I confessed.

"That's understandable, sweetie, and I'm sorry you had to do this alone, but you won't be alone for long. Zayvion is gonna beat this bullshit and then everything will be alright," Dara replied reassuringly.

Again, she spoke with a confidence and passion I didn't understand because there was no way she knew something I didn't. We hadn't been apart since I'd dropped the news about Zay in her lap, so I knew she didn't call to find some shit out. Still, she had a look in her eyes like she believed every word she spoke.

"I hope you're right, because little Zayvion is gonna need his daddy around," I admitted.

While Dara tended to the clean-up in between my legs, I took my time inspecting my son thoroughly, counting his little fingers and toes.

"You're perfect Zay-Zay," I whispered, kissing his tiny face.

By the time I passed the placenta and Dara had given me the three stitches my pussy required, the ambulance was there to take us to the hospital. Considering that I'd already given birth I don't see the need for a hospital run, but Dara wasn't hearing it. I protested about having to leave my car when I had nobody to come get it, and she offered to drive it to the hospital for me. The bitch had an answer for everything! I couldn't deny that I was grateful though, because the reality that I was out here all alone with four kids now, was settling in on me real quick like. As I was being loaded into the ambulance, I again found myself yearning for the husband I thought I no longer wanted or needed. The proof of my lie was fast asleep on my chest, and it was inspiring a mantra in my head that was screaming for me to get Zayvion out! If only it was that easy though. Instead of basking in the glory of my beautiful baby boy, I spent the ride to the hospital in deep thought, trying to figure out how to still achieve the ultimate goal, while getting Zay out immediately. Did I want to have my cake and eat it too? God damn right, and I wanted ice cream on top! Sadly, I didn't see a way to make that happen. After we got checked in and my little man was whisked away to receive a check-up, I set about the business of putting my life back together. The first thing I did was text the babysitter and let her know what had happened so she could make the necessary arrangements to stay with the kids until I got back. Thankfully, we'd had this plan ready once I knew Zay wouldn't be around. I knew that was my easy phone call, because now I had to tread carefully into the deep waters.

"Hi, I need to speak to you if you have time," I said, when the phone was answered.

"Actually, you caught me in the car, so we can talk now. I'm sorry I had to leave so abruptly earlier but uh, something came up," Charles replied.

"You know, for you to be such a great lawyer, Mr. Swedish, you lie terribly sometimes. Tell me what Zayvion did."

"That's not why you called, Carmen, so we don't—"

"You're right, I called you because I want you to get him out, but I'm still his wife and I wanna know what happened," I said quickly.

"He, uh, got into a fight."

"You wouldn't be acting jittery over a fight, so how bad did Zay hurt the guy?" I asked.

The silence following my question was thick, but it was definitely loud too.

"That bad, huh? Well, will it stop you from getting him a bond?" I asked.

"I thought you didn't want me to worry about another bond hearing."

"Yeah, well that was before I went into labor and had my son a little while ago," I replied, marveling at how quickly everything can and did change.

"Congratulations, Carmen! I know Zayvion is in the hole, but I'll tell him if you want me to when I go visit him at Powhatan in a few days."

"Powhatan? He's back in prison already? Wow, he must've fucked dude up! No, Charles, I don't want you to tell him. I just want you to get him out," I said emphatically.

"I understand, but despite my earlier comments about believing that Zayvion was set up, all I can do at this point is file another motion for bond. And honestly, because of his violation, I doubt any judge will give him a bond."

"Charles, listen to me. Zay was absolutely set up and you have to get him out, because I need him home," I stated calmly.

"Can you prove that he was set up?"

Now it was my turn to go silent, because unless I was gonna go to the police station and give a full confession, Zayvion was stuck. I may have been in my feelings, but I wasn't falling on my own sword.

"I know your emotions are all over the place right now, but I'm gonna need you to trust me to do everything I can for Zayvion. I'll file the motion for a bail hearing on Monday, okay? Is that soon enough, or do you need me to make a surprise visit?"

"No, that's soon enough. Charles, thank you. We do still need to get together and discuss those changes you said Zay put into place. Can I come by on Monday?" I asked.

"Tuesday would be better."

"Okay, I'll see you Tuesday then," I said, hanging up the phone, feeling defeated.

I hadn't thought my decision to give Zayvion a taste of his own medicine was one I'd made on impulse, but I definitely didn't feel like I'd thought it through now. I hadn't forgiven him for his betrayals, but I hadn't stopped loving him either. Right now, I was at war with myself and I was getting my ass kicked. I sent Abby a text, letting her know the latest tea in my life and asked her to pass it on, before I was forced to succumb to my exhaustion and sleep. I wasn't plagued by dreams or nightmares, but there was a vague feeling of unease that hovered around me. When I woke up I had the same feeling, but everything around me seemed to be as it should. I noticed it was dark outside and when I looked at my phone, I saw it was two a.m., and Abby had been blowing my phone up for the last three and a half hours. I quickly dialed her number, trying to fight my feeling of unease that was rapidly growing.

"Ab, what's wrong?" I asked, as soon as she answered.

"They moved, Rocko! There was no warning and no reason, they just moved him!" She replied, distressed.

"Abby calm down, you're pregnant, and trust me that stress ain't good for my niece. We knew Rocko would be transferred eventually, so—"

"Carmen, this move wasn't regular! They got him after ten p.m. count, and he was taken away in a van," she said, fighting not to panic.

"Where did they take him?"

"Sussex One State Prison," she replied.

Zayvion had never made it to that spot, but I knew it was pretty high on the custody level and that wasn't abnormal, given Rocko's time and charge. I had a sneaky suspicion about why they'd moved him now though.

"Abby, it's okay. I think I know why they moved him. It's because Zayvion is there and for obvious reasons they don't want them around each other," I said.

"But, Rocko was okay with being around Zayvion. He even had me take him a note and—"

"Wait, you saw Zayvion?" I asked quickly.

"Y-yeah, but only for a couple minutes. I didn't want to go near him, especially after hearing he beat a dude almost half to death today, but Rocko wanted me to go see him."

"How was he? I mean, is he okay?" I asked, hoping my voice sounded neutral.

"He was fine. For him to be such a monster, he was surprisingly polite and soft spoken."

"He's not a monster, Abby, where did you get that impression?" I asked.

Her silence was as good as saying Rocko's name and I could understand her biased opinion.

"Listen, my brother and Zay are just at odds right now, but I promise you Zay would never hurt you. He's not like that. He did what he had to do in the street, but he won't hurt a woman," I said reassuringly.

"Do you think they moved Rocko because Zay was gonna hurt him?"

"No, they moved Rocko because of Zay's involvement in Rocko's case. It's documented and so the state had to cover their ass by not having them around each other," I replied.

"So then, how is this plan gonna work? How are they gonna escape if they're not at the same prison? Carmen, I need Rocko home, I don't want to raise our daughter by myself," she said, getting excited again.

For a moment I had to bite my tongue, because hearing this bitch complain about raising one kid alone, while I was now a single mother to four was about to get her cussed all the way out.

"Didn't I tell you to calm down? Zayvion will figure the shit out, don't worry," I replied.

"How can you be so sure?"

"Because he loves his freedom and his kids too much to willingly spend the rest of his life in prison. He'll do what he has to, even if he doesn't like it," I replied confidently.

"God, I hope you're right. I still don't know what I should do now though, because it's gonna look strange if I suddenly quit working here, and go get a job where they moved Rocko to."

"You're right and that's why you're not gonna do that. Your being there allows you to keep tabs on Zayvion, so we can make sure he's going along with the game plan," I said.

"But-but what if he knows I'm spying on him and he hurts me, or—"

"Abby, didn't I just tell you he won't hurt you? I know my husband and I know what he's capable of. I wouldn't put you or my niece in danger, okay? All you have to do is act natural and don't go sneaking around like you're trying to spy on him. Get him to trust you. Matter of fact, I want you to go see him and give him a message for me. I want you to tell him I'm sorry it had to be this way, but I love him and want him home, so he needs to do the right thing," I said.

"Are you sure?"

"Yeah, I'm sure. Tell him to call me too, because I have something important to tell him," I replied.

"Okay, I'll do it, but I hope you're right," she said, skeptically.

"I'm right, trust me. Call me tomorrow, okay?"

"I will and thanks, Carmen," she replied, hanging up.

I took a long deep breath, thankful I'd managed to avoid Abby having a complete breakdown, because that was the last thing I needed. What I needed right now was to see my son, and with that thought in mind, I hit my nurse's call button.

"You seem positively convinced Zayvion will be out sooner than later," a voice said, from the shadows of the corner behind my hospital room door. The fact that I jumped was involuntary, but I had no doubt the look on my face was like every white girl's in a scary movie.

"Who the fuck are you?" I asked, wishing I had a gun in my hand right now.

"Me? Oh, my name is Shmurda. I'm Jesha's cousin."

Aryanna

Chapter 6

Rocko

Three days later

By the time they'd announced stand-by for breakfast, I'd already been awake for almost two hours, staring into the darkness of my cell looking for answers. I knew I should've anticipated the Department of Corrections wanting to keep me and Zay apart, but I hadn't and so I was still trying to recover from the monkey wrench thrown into the plans. This new spot was damn near max security, which made everything harder. Nothing was impossible though, I just had to be patient. That didn't come easy to me, especially now that Abby wasn't on the inside with me. My first instinct had been to have her transfer her position out here, but after she relayed the conversation she'd had with Carmen, I was forced to begrudgingly acknowledge that it was smart for her to stay put. The inconvenience of me having to do hard time for the moment, didn't compare to the greater good that had to be accomplished. The fact that Carmen had given birth to my nephew by herself had given Abby a harsh reality check, and now I could hear the fear in her voice every time we spoke. I hated that! True enough, we were both consenting adults who knew the risks we were taking by fucking without protection, but I hated Abby was now trapped in a life of fear that was a result of her decision to be with me. I'd never stop feeling like she was too good for me and this situation, even though I understood we'd come too far to go back.

"Damn, did you sleep in your clothes?" my celly asked, chuckling after he'd turned on the light and spotted me sitting up in bed.

"Nah, I've been up for a little while but don't worry. I wasn't watching you sleep," I replied.

So far, the only good thing that had come from my transfer was that they'd put me in the cell with a mufucka that was okay.

Everybody called him Pittsburgh, because that's where he was from, but he still got respect out here. That was a rare thing for a white boy, but he moved with a certain kind of swag that allowed him to move and shake with anybody.

"You watching me sleep wouldn't be weird at all," he said, sarcastically.

"Right, right, right. Are you going to breakfast?" I asked, putting my shoes on because I heard doors opening.

"Yeah, I need those pancakes."

"You better hurry your ass up then," I said, moving by the door because I knew I'd have to keep it from closing while he got dressed.

I got a surprise though, because when our door finally opened, it was two mangy-looking white boys standing there waiting.

"We need to holla at your celly," the taller of the two said.

I'd been around long enough to immediately recognize these two mufuckas weren't at the door this early in the morning for no type of conversation.

"Yo, Pittsburgh, do you know these dudes?" I asked, not taking my eyes off of either one.

"Get the fuck away from my door, I ain't got no dope for you," Pittsburgh said.

"Fuck you, whore, we'll run up in that motherfucker—"

That was as far as the tall dude got with his three, before I grabbed him by his shirt and pulled him in the cell. I didn't hit him though. I pushed him behind me to Pittsburgh so I could grab his partner and invite him to the party. He tried to hold onto the door jam, but I head-butted him in the nose, and that forced him to use his hands like a bucket to catch the blood that was raining fast. He had a stunned look on his face, but it quickly morphed into one of terror when he heard the door lock behind him. I wasted no time firing a left/right combo that made his lip get bigger and his eye get smaller, and he wisely chose to ball up. When I looked behind me I was just in time to see Pittsburgh lift his man off his feet with a solid upper cut. Once he hit the ground, Pittsburgh put the boots to him, and I turned back to my man so I could follow his lead. I could tell by their pleas this was the longest thirty seconds of their life, but they were gonna learn today!

"If you bitches ever come to my cell again you won't leave alive," Pittsburgh warned.

"Shut up all that damn crying," I said, pushing the button for the intercom on the wall that connected to the guard tower.

"Yes?" a female asked immediately.

"We're going to eat," I said calmly.

The intercom clicked off and our door slid open again. Luckily, there was still enough traffic in the pod to get these mufuckas out in a hurry.

"Get the fuck out," I said, kicking the dude I'd beat up in the ass.

Both men scrambled to their feet and fled as fast as their legs would carry them.

"Pancakes?" I asked, looking at Pittsburgh.

"Pancakes," he replied, smiling.

I was careful not to step in the blood on our floor, because tracking that through the building would bring all types of questions I didn't need. I didn't think the two white boys would go to the cops because they'd been in our cell, and no excuse given would justify that rule violation. Basically that just meant we had to keep our eyes open for them to make a move against us.

"So, what was that about?" I asked, once we were seated with our trays in the chow hall.

"The tall dude's name is Slim, but I think his real name is Hurst or something. The dude's ass you whooped is named Kersee. Long story short is that they're cellies, junkies, and fuck buddies, and they both have a weird obsession with seven-year-old little girls. All around they're the lowest of the low because they're both rats too. Kersee is good at making shit out of wood, like jewelry boxes, clocks, model cars, that type of shit. He likes to work for dope, and I did business with him before, but it didn't turn out right so I chalked him for what I owed him. He tried sending his celly to get something from me, but I chalked him too. I guess they called themselves pushing on me this morning, but they didn't see shit going the way it did. I appreciate your assistance by the way," he replied.

"It's nothing, I didn't like their tone. Do we gotta worry about retaliation?"

"Not unless you wanna get your dick sucked, because both of them will do that through the slot in the door for a little piece of Saboxin," he replied, laughing.

"Nah, I'm good on that."

"Them motherfuckers ain't nobody and they ain't worth another thought, especially when you've got other shit to think about," he said, smiling mischievously.

"What are you talking about?" I asked cautiously.

"All I'ma say is that I know how to return a favor and trust me, you'll love it."

I had no idea what he was talking about, but I evaluated him a little different than I had a few days ago. The short brown hair, bushy beard, and glasses made him seem unassuming, but I was beginning to understand his mind was always playing the angles. A dude like that could make a powerful ally or a formidable enemy.

"Whatever you say, bruh," I replied, going back to my pancakes.

We managed to eat breakfast and make it back to our pod without any more bullshit and since this morning's visitors had been his guests, Pittsburgh offered to clean the cell. We were only allowed two hours of rec a day, not counting the hour we got outside, so even though it was only 6:30 a.m. the poker table was already open for business. After grabbing a few dollars' worth of commissary I found me a seat, and prepared to waste some time. It wasn't like I didn't have plenty of it to waste! The thing that sucked about having to transfer to a different prison was having to start over. Being with Abby at Powhatan had given me access to everything I needed, and now I just felt naked. Somehow, someway, I was gonna have to reestablish order and get comfortable again.

"I gotta go to medical, but the cell is straight," Pittsburgh whispered in my ear.

I nodded my head and went back to watching the cards turn. Before I knew it, I'd won fifty dollars in food and hygiene, but my hot streak was stopped by outside rec being called. Given the choice of being locked in my cell or going to play basketball, I chose the latter and put all my stuff in my cell. I'd almost made it out the door when the guard in the tower summoned me and handed me a pass that read I was to report directly to medical. My frustration was real because they would pick now to need me, versus when I was stuck in my cell twiddling my damn thumbs! It would be too much like right for the people employed by the state to do some shit that made sense, so I resigned myself to my fate and headed for medical. When I got to the holding area and saw all the people waiting, I only got madder because I was missing my rec for no reason, if all these mufuckas were in front of me. My anger was short-lived though, because as soon as I handed the C.O., my pass, he buzzed the two doors necessary for me to get into medical.

"Last name?" a nurse behind a desk asked.

"Vargas"

"Go on back to exam room three, that'll be the third door on your right," she instructed.

I followed her directions, but found the room empty when I got there, so I took a seat on the table.

"So, you're Mr. Vargas," a nurse said, coming into the room and closing the door behind her.

I could tell right away she was young, but she was a cute white girl. She had brown hair with blonde highlights, stood about five foot six, and she was a doable hundred and seventy pounds.

"Yes, I'm Mr. Vargas, and you are?"

"Oh, I'm Shelby," she replied, putting her hand out for me to shake.

The gesture caught me off guard, but I took her hand anyway. When I didn't immediately let it go, she blushed a shade of red I'd only seen on fire engines.

"Nice to meet you, Shelby," I said smiling.

"Y-you too. So, tell me about yourself."

"Huh?" I asked, confused.

"You know. Tell me who you are and what you like. I need to know more than just what your file says."

"Why do I get the feeling you're not talking about my medical history?" I asked slowly.

Her laughter was instantaneous and bubbly, and it made her green eyes dance in a way that was effortlessly sexy. This girl was trouble with all capital letters.

"Of course I'm not talking about your medical history, Rocko, I wanna get to know this great guy that Pittsburgh spent the last hour telling me about."

"Pittsburgh told you about me, huh?" I asked, putting the pieces together finally.

"Yeah, he's my mom's boyfriend, even though my mom is technically still married to my dad. I don't judge, I just want her to be happy, plus who wants to live with bad sex?"

The expression on her face when she asked that question made me laugh.

"You're crazy," I said, shaking my head.

"Oh trust me, you have no idea."

I didn't think she meant for that to sound as sexy as it did, but I could tell she was comfortable with letting the innuendo hang in the air.

"So, you want to know about me? How much time do we have?" I asked.

"At least two hours. My mom runs shit over here so she'll make it all look legit, but we have to talk in low tones so others don't overhear."

"Well, hop up here and let me whisper to you," I said, patting the spot beside me on the exam table.

She accepted my challenge without hesitation, and so it began. We weren't fifteen minutes into the conversation, before I realized I had the ability to mentally run laps around this twenty-two-year-old girl, because it was obvious she'd never met a nigga like me.

The fact that she still lived at home, even though she made good money was a testament to her sheltered upbringing, but I was okay with that. I was gonna be the nigga to turn her out though. I kept up the conversation and picked her brain, while flirting with her in a way I was almost positive no man had ever done before. I waited for the perfect opportunity and then I closed the trap with a kiss that was tender as it was passionate.

"Wow," she sighed when I finally pulled back and let her breathe again.

"I've wanted to do that for the last thirty minutes, I confessed.

"Then you waited twenty-nine minutes too long," she replied, practically hopping in my lap as her lips found mine with a fierce hunger.

I let loose with my mouth skills, making my tongue dance with hers in an electrifying seduction. When I slipped my hand inside her pants and panties I could feel her heat, but when I pushed my middle finger inside her tight pussy, it felt like it'd stuck my hand in a glass of water.

"Are you a virgin?" I asked.

"No, but I'll take that as a compliment," she replied, grinding on my finger.

She may not have been a virgin, but she was absolutely sexually frustrated. When I brought a second finger into the mix, her pussy clamped down like it had teeth, making my dick painfully hard. But, I knew what I had to do before indulging in my own pleasure.

"I want you," I said seductively.

"Y-you can have me."

The pure submission in her voice was making it hard for me to concentrate, but I stayed focused.

"I want you now," I said, pulling back so I could look at her.

Her eyes were swimming in lust, and what I had in mind would make her drown.

"You want me now. Okay. What do you want? Do you wanna cum on my face?" she asked.

"What? Why would you ask me that?"

"I just thought, well most guys tell me I have that porn star face, the one that's good for the money shot," she replied honestly.

There was so much I wanted to say, but I knew my actions would speak louder than words.

"I'm not most guys," I said, kissing her softly on both of her cheeks, and then once again on her lips.

When I pulled my fingers from inside her, I could tell she had questions, but I put a finger to her lips to silence her. I got down off the table and stood in front of her.

"Lift up," I said, grabbing her pants and panties, pulling them down over her hips.

She quickly kicked her legs free so that she was naked from the waist down, and she scooted to the edge of the table. I took a seat on the doctor's stool, putting me eye level with her nicely trimmed pussy, and before she could ask what I was doing, my tongue was deep inside her. The gasp that escaped her mouth sounded panicked, but we both knew it was too late now. She was lost. I took my time tasting her, becoming completely familiar with her most intimate of intimates before latching onto her clit. She'd done a good job of keeping her moaning low so we wouldn't be overheard, but when I started sucking on that clit she lost if for a second.

"Shhh, baby, it's okay," I said, putting one of her legs on each of my shoulders, allowing her to wrap herself around me.

And that's what she did, quicker than a boa constrictor. Within minutes, I had her cum and pussy juices quenching my thirst while she battled mightily to control her sounds of passion. A sudden knock at the door froze my tongue in mid-lick.

"Shelby? You almost finished?" a woman's voice called out.

"Y-yeah, Mom, just a couple-couple more minutes," she replied shakily.

"Okay, sweetie."

I didn't dare move until I heard her walk away.

"Well, I guess that concludes—"

"No, no, it don't conclude shit! Fuck me, Rocko, fuck me now!" she demanded, pulling me towards her.

Before I knew it, she had my dick out and she was wrapping her legs around me, pulling me inside her. I could tell by the expression on her face and her harsh breathing that she hadn't had this much dick in this tight little pussy before, but she wasn't backing away from it. I gave her a few strokes to get used to it, and then I showed her what she'd been missing. Even with my hand firmly clamped over her mouth, I still felt like she was too damn loud, but the pussy was too good to stop. I fucked her fast and hard, lifting her off the table with the power behind my blows. Within a couple minutes, her body was shaking like she'd swallowed an earthquake, drenching me with the sweet scent of her orgasm. That only made me fuck her harder. I was pounding dick inside her like I was angry with her, and the way she clung to me proved that she loved every inch of it. By now her pussy was sloppy wet, and the sound every time I dove deep was like a water balloon fight. I could tell by the way she was gripping me inside and out that the aftershocks she was feeling were about to give way to another systemic shift, forcing me to move faster and fling us both off the cliff of ecstasy. It hadn't been my intention to cum inside her, but there was no way I could've pulled out. We clung to each other, sucking in much-needed oxygen as our bodies tried to cool down. Somehow my lips found hers again and this time when I moved inside, I did it slowly.

"I know we don't have time right now, but next time I'll be gentle," I said softly.

"As long as you make me cum like that, you can do anything you want to me. Do you want me to bring you anything? I know my mom brings Pittsburgh food all the time. I'll bring whatever, even drugs," she whispered, smiling at me.

"I don't want you to get into trouble, baby, or get fired, so let's take things slow. Some home cooked food would be nice though, so then I can feel like we're on a date."

"I'll do it tomorrow. What do you want to eat?" she asked.

"As long as you're on the menu too, I don't care. I do need you to bring me one other thing though."

"Anything," she said quickly.

"I need you to bring me the layout of this prison, and every-thing in a five-mile radius."

Chapter 7

Zay

"How are you holding up?" Charles asked, sitting down across from me.

"You know I'm used to this shit, but it's kinda different when I've done absolutely nothing to be here."

"Yeah, I told Carmen I thought you were too smart to let yourself get caught up like that, even if you had done it. She agrees you were set up," he replied.

"How nice of her to believe in my innocence," I said sarcastically.

"She still loves you, Zayvion."

"It's funny, you're the second person to tell me that recently," I replied.

"You almost sound like you don't believe it. I'm sure she confessed her undying love for you, especially with how high her emotions were running when I last spoke to her."

"I haven't talked to Carmen yet, but I'm sure I'll get around to it eventually. Right now, we need to discuss—"

"Wait, so you haven't spoken to your wife at all?" he asked suddenly.

"No, why?"

The way he hesitated when I asked that question gave me a bad feeling.

"I just think you need to call her ASAP. Did they move you out of the hole yet?" he asked.

"They moved me this morning, but don't try to change the subject or avoid my question. Why are you so insistent that I call Carmen?"

"Because she had the baby," he blurted out.

"My son-my son was born? When?" I asked weakly.

"Friday, not long after your court appearance, I think. He's fine though and so is she, but I know she needs to hear from you.

When I last spoke to her, she was insisting that I get you a bond and move every mountain, because she needed you home now."

Hearing my son had been born without me there to welcome him into the world caused an emotional fog to cloud my brain, but that quickly cleared when Charles told me all that Carmen had said. Through the fog came rage.

"She needs me home, huh?" I asked calmly.

"Yeah, I'm going to file a new bond motion when I leave here. I just needed to get your approval."

"No, it's a waste of time and money. By any chance, did you tell Carmen about the changes I'd put in place?" I asked.

"Not specifically, she's supposed to come to the office tomorrow so we can discuss everything."

"I don't want you to discuss anything with her, but I do want you to keep your appointment with her. By then, I want you to have my divorce papers drawn up so you can serve her in person," I said.

"D-divorce papers? Come on, Zayvion, you don't think she'd react that badly to you making me the power of attorney over all of your money and assets, so you? I mean, you can simply explain you did it in case the law came after her too, and with me having control it prevents them from freezing or taking anything."

"This ain't about that, Charles, it's so much deeper. Just get it done," I demanded.

"Okay. What do you want to do about the kids?"

"Joint custody and I'll pay child support for my three kids, but Rocko can take care of his own son," I replied.

"Zayvion, are you sure about this? I mean, I know you and Carmen have had your ups and downs, but you two love each other. If you do this, you know you'll be leaving her with only whatever she squirreled away."

"Trust me, Carmen's pockets ain't hurting in the slightest, and my only concern is that my kids are taken care of. She'll get fifteen thousand dollars a month, and she can stay in the house she's living in now. If she needs more than that, tell her to get a job," I replied dispassionately.

"O-kay. Speaking of houses, what do you want me to do with the one you bought Iesha? The cops have officially finished with it."

"Don't do anything right now. If they're finished gathering bullshit evidence, when is my next court date?" I asked.

"A month from now we have your preliminary hearing, which isn't a lot of time for me to build a defense, so you need to tell me how we're going at this thing," he replied, opening his briefcase and pulling out his note pad.

"It's simple, I didn't do it. I loved Iesha and she'd just given birth to my son, so why would I kill her?"

"Do you have an alibi?" he asked.

"Actually I do, but I don't know if she's gonna agree to testify. It's complicated."

"As soon as you said the word *she,* I knew it was complicated. Who's the lucky girl this time?" he asked, shaking his head.

"The woman who just delivered my son."

"Wait a minute, you're fucking your wife's doctor?" he asked in disbelief.

"Stop judging me, Charles, I had to get Carmen the best doctor available and I had to be persuasive," I rationalized.

"O-kay. Well, do you want to call the good doctor or should I?"

"I'll handle it, but if she's not willing to testify then we've gotta think of something else," I replied.

"How far apart does the doctor live from Iesha, and how long were you two together?"

"She stays a couple hours away, and I was with her all weekend. Her name is Dara Silver," I said.

"Okay, well your Cadillac isn't exactly inconspicuous, so hopefully we'll get some traffic cam footage. It's circumstantial, but they need twelve and we only need one. Let's discuss your DNA inside Iesha and the trauma to her, uh, lady parts."

"The trauma was part of the set-up because we didn't have rough sex like that, or at least not rough enough to damage the pussy. Of course my cum would be in her, because I fucked her regularly," I replied.

"When was the last time you were with her?" he asked.

"Right before I spent the weekend with Dara."

"Alright, well I won't know her time of death until I get the discovery packet. I'm gonna be honest with you though, Zayvion, our best bet is that you convince the good doctor to come to the rescue. You gotta remember you're not just being prosecuted for this case, but for the one you walked away from less than a year ago. That loss still burns the state's ass because they thought they had you boxed in, so you better believe they're gonna try and nail your ass to the cross this time around," he stated seriously.

"Yeah, I know. I'll work on shit on my end and you do the same on yours. I'll call you when I need you to come back up here," I replied, standing up.

"Okay. Your violation hearing should be in a couple of weeks, but I'll let you know the exact date."

We shook hands and then I signaled the C.O. to let me out. As I made my way back to the housing unit where new intakes had to stay, I contemplated all that my lawyer and I had just discussed. Truthfully, I should've been single-minded with my focus being on obtaining my freedom, but my thoughts circled around Carmen like a song I couldn't get out of my head. Now knowing that my son had been born helped to put Abby's surprise late night visit into context. The fact that Abby had come back to see me at all was shocking, and I'd had my doubts about whether it had been Carmen or Rocko who sent her, but now I knew. It sounded like Carmen was having regrets, but it was too late for that shit. It was all out war from now on.

"Damn, I was hoping mufuckas was lying about you being back."

I immediately recognized the voice and I fixed my face on the fitting expression.

"Shit's crazy, Cuzzo, but it's good to see you regardless," I replied, smiling and embracing him like we'd never missed a beat.

"I heard you was in the hole."

"Yeah, I melted a nigga in the hall after my arraignment, but when he regained consciousness, he didn't remember what happened," I replied.

"Damn, you beat him like that?"

"Of course I did, disrespect will not be tolerated," I said, looking at him pointedly.

"Yeah, I feel that. Your man was just here, but they shipped him to Sussex One. I knew you was gonna take a look at him personally."

"Without a doubt. It's very personal between him and me, even though he recanted his testimony," I replied.

"Oh, so that's how you got out."

"The only way to get out was to beat the charges, you know that, bruh," I said, watching his face closely.

I could tell he wasn't fully believing the simple explanation I'd given, but he knew to ask anything else would surely get him fucked up.

"Where are you coming from?" he asked, smoothly switching subjects.

"My lawyer came to see me. What about you?"

"Medical. I'm going back to the pod though and I've got some shit for you," he said.

"Who's working up there?"

"Burnette, so you good," he said, leading the way to the stairway.

I didn't have on the right color jumpsuit, but the C.O. in the downstairs booth wasn't paying attention, so I followed Hambone's lead.

"You go grab whatever you got while I holla at Burnette," I said, stopping just out of view of anyone on the floor.

Once Ham had passed through the gate, I flagged Burnette down and she quickly came out of the booth.

"Oh, my God, Zayvion! I've been looking for you, what the fuck happened?" she asked, in a fierce whisper.

"It's a long story, but the short version is that I got framed for Iesha's murder."

"Who set you up?" she asked immediately.

"My soon to be ex-wife, but don't worry because I'm dealing with all that. I need your help on something else."

"Anything, just name it," she replied.

I quickly laid out my plan for her, making sure to talk low so no one except us would hear it.

"Are you sure you'll be able to get out at that time?" she asked, once I'd explained everything.

"Yeah, I'll be there. Are you sure you're okay going along with my plan?"

"I trust that you wouldn't go to this extreme if you didn't think it was necessary, so I'm with you. You gotta do something for me though," she said.

"What do you need?"

Before I knew what was happening, she'd pushed me into the hallway where we were both completely out of sight, and her lips were on mine with a ferocious hunger. I grabbed two handfuls of her juicy ass and lifted her into the air like she weighed no more than a feather, and I kissed her with the same passion. It was clear what she wanted and needed but now wasn't the time or place, so I put her back on her feet after a solid sixty seconds of tongue action.

"So, I guess you missed me, huh?" I asked, smiling down at her.

"Boy, you have no idea! And it's not like I can't get dick if I wanted it, but I'm yours and that means something to me. I only want your dick, so are you gonna give it to me or what?"

"The first chance I get, sweetheart. I promise," I said, kissing her lips gently.

"I'm gonna hold you to that, and I'll do what you asked tonight. Would you be mad if I pulled some strings and got you moved back on this floor?"

"Not as long as you can do it without bringing attention to yourself," I replied.

"I can do it. I'll just say that I need you to do the floors over here, because I'm familiar with your work from when you were last here."

"You're familiar with me waxing, as in that ass," I said, laughing.

"Ha-ha, funny man, you just be ready to move in the next few days."

"Burnette?" Ham called from the gate.

We shared one last passionate kiss and then I let her go so she could let him out.

"Aight, bruh, I got you a bunch of food, and here's a half-ounce of weed too," Ham said, passing me a net bag and a Ziploc bag.

I quickly tucked the weed into my boxers before slinging the bag of groceries over my shoulder.

"I appreciate it, bruh. I'ma get on out of here, but I'll see you later."

I tossed a wink at Burnette before quickly making my way back downstairs. I moved like I was street legal, which allowed me to make it all the way to my cell without being stopped. Once I had the weed stashed and the food put away, I covered the window so I could pull out the phone Alexis had brought me a couple days ago. I knew she wouldn't be at work until tonight, so I sent her a text saying we needed to talk. She called me immediately, and I told her exactly what I needed her to do for me. She agreed, but I could tell she was disappointed by the fact that this meant we wouldn't be fucking tonight. I did manage to talk her into playing with that pussy until she was moaning my name breathlessly, and I promised I'd serve her this dick real soon. After our call was over, I actually contemplated calling Carmen, but the time for our conversation would come soon enough. Instead, I put my phone up, broke out a few grams of weed for my next transaction, and then I got about the business of what I needed taken care of.

Despite all the chaos in my life, the day still seemed to pass with ease. Before I knew it, it was lockdown time in preparation for ten p.m. count, but I was preparing mentally for my next move.

Once count cleared, I made sure I was dressed and ready, so when the C.O. suddenly appeared at my door to take me for my breathing treatment I hopped up without hesitation. Because it was after lockdown, inmates had to be escorted everywhere within the prison, but Alexis told the young dude escorting me that I would be there at least an hour. He agreed to just come back and get me, which was what I'd been hoping for. At eleven p.m., Alexis called upstairs to talk to Burnette, who'd volunteered to work a double, and asked her to escort my cousin down to medical. I waited exactly three minutes after that call before I walked out of medical and made my way to the stairway. Once I was there, I slipped on a pair of latex gloves and waited.

"Why am I going to medical?" I heard Ham ask a few minutes later.

"I don't know, I was just told to escort you," Burnette replied.

"Well damn, since we've got a moment alone, why don't you let me give you some of this dope dick?" Ham suggested.

"I told you before, I'm not interested in all that, so—"

"Oh, but you'll fuck with my snitchin' ass cousin!" he said hotly.

They had just come into view as he'd made this statement and I could see the smirk on Burnette's face. I pulled the eight-inch shank from the waist of my pants and moved like I was walking on cotton. He never saw it coming until it was too late. With the swiftness of a viper, I stabbed him twice in the right side of his neck and stood over him as he stared at me in shock and horror, while blood poured between his fingers. In the movies, this would be the perfect time for a witty one-liner, but I had no words for this nigga. We were closer than brothers, but Rocko had taught me why no one should ever be allowed that close, and that wasn't a lesson I was soon to forget. Once he collapsed to the floor with that faraway look in his eyes, I passed the knife to Burnette.

"You know the story, right?" I asked.

"He tried to rape me at knife point, but I got the upper hand."

"Did you take care of the cameras in the hallway outside this door?" I asked.

"And the ones on the hallway to medical. Nothing will come back on until I hit my panic button."

"Wait forty-five seconds and then hit the button," I said, peeling off my gloves and giving her a quick kiss.

"I love you," she blurted out.

"I know," I replied, kissing her once again before I opened the door and walked out.

My steps weren't hurried and I'd just made it back to the exam room Alexis was in, when I heard the thunder of footsteps racing down the hallway.

"Everything good?" Alexis asked.

"No, but it's getting there."

Aryanna

Chapter 8

Carmen

"I'm sorry I'm late, Charles, but having two newborns is kicking my ass. I had to hire my baby sitter as the live-in nanny until further notice, so I hope you're about to tell me that you've worked a miracle to get Zay home," I said, flopping down in the soft leather chair across from him.

I could immediately tell he was uneasy, but I wasn't sure why yet.

"I'm sorry, Carmen, no miracles yet."

"What about bond? When is his next court date for that, because I'll show up with all the kids and convince the judge my goddamn self!" I said seriously.

"Zayvion didn't want me to file another motion for bond. He said he wanted me focused on other things."

"Other things like what? What's more important than trying to secure his freedom as soon as possible?" I asked, fighting my own frustration.

"Preparing for his trial for one thing and…"

"And what? Spit it out," I prompted once he'd gone silent.

I could see the dread all over his face as he grabbed some papers off his desk and handed them to me. When I saw the words *petition for divorce* in bold letters, I laughed out loud because I thought it was a joke, but then I saw mine and Zayvion's names. Seeing that stopped shit from being funny real quick.

"You're fucking with me, right? I know that nigga didn't tell you to draw up no fucking divorce papers," I said, becoming angrier with each passing second.

"Yeah, he did. Carmen, I swear, I tried to talk him out of it—"

"The nerve of this nigga! He gets another bitch pregnant and has the balls to ask me for a goddamn divorce?" I yelled, hopping up out of my seat.

"Carmen, please calm down. You know Zayvion is a hot head and once he gets over whatever he's mad about, there will be no more talk of divorce, so all you gotta do—"

"Nah, fuck that! If he wants a divorce, I'll give him one and I'll leave his black ass penniless, while he rots in prison!" I said spitefully.

"Carmen, listen to me before you pick a fight you can't win. Zayvion loves you and—"

"Oh, I can win, and you're a good enough lawyer to know that. What judge in America wouldn't award me everything Zay has, especially with me having to provide for his kids?" I asked.

"Zayvion said he'd give you fifteen thousand a month, plus you can keep the house you're living in."

"Awww, how nice, but you can tell that motherfucker I'm taking it all," I replied, smiling despite being furious.

"Carmen, please listen to me, you can't win."

As I was opening my mouth to argue just how easily I would win, I noticed the expression on the face of the seasoned attorney, and I paused.

"Charles, why can't I win?" I asked cautiously.

I could tell that whatever was about to come out of his mouth wasn't good, at least not for me.

"You can't win because Zayvion doesn't have any assets or money for you to take. He had everything moved and appointed a new power of attorney, just in case the feds ever came at both of you at the same time. It was done to protect you, but now it protects him."

"Who-who is his power of attorney?" I asked weakly.

"I'm not at liberty to say."

As the reality of what I'd just been told set in I sat down, feeling like all the wind had been knocked out of me. Zayvion knew I had little formal education and no job experience, so why would he leave me for dead? There was no need to voice this question out loud or even waste time contemplating it because the answer was as simple as this being payback. Maybe I should've seen this coming, but even after I'd done what I did I never really thought

Zay and I would be over. We had too much history, we had kids and—"

"The baby! He wouldn't have asked for a divorce if he knew I had his son," I said quickly.

"He knows. I had to tell him so that he was making an informed decision."

"He-he knows about the baby, and he still told you to file that paperwork?" I asked in disbelief.

"I'm so sorry, Carmen, I really am."

A big part of me wanted to scream until I passed out from lock of oxygen, but I didn't see how that was gonna help my situation. Of course I had money put away because I was the wife of a hustla, so I never had to spend what he gave me. It wasn't about the money though. Zayvion was cutting me out of his life in a very permanent way, and that terrified me most of all. I could be broke, busted, and disgusted as long as my man loved me enough to go through it with me, but the papers I was still clutching in my hand signified that he didn't love me no more. How was that even possible?

"I need to hear all of this from his mouth," I said.

"He said he'd call you eventually, so—"

"No, we're gonna handle this today, and you're gonna help," I said, standing up.

"I am?"

"Yes, Charles, you are. I'm gonna go home and change into something a paralegal would wear, and you're gonna schedule us a visit at the prison," I stated calmly.

"But Carmen, your name alone—"

"You know I've got good fake papers, so save your arguments. I'll be back in one hour," I said, turning and leaving before he could put up any more of a fight.

There was no way I was just gonna let Zayvion ignore me while he played puppet master from his prison cell. I was too real of a bitch to be treated like that and he was gonna have to face me today. I hopped in my truck, tossing the divorce papers on the passenger seat, and thought about what I would wear as I started the engine and pulled off. If I could somehow put this pussy on him, I know I could convince him to give us another try, but that might be asking too much to have the lawyer arrange that. If push came to shove, I'd just have to be an exhibitionist for today. I made the drive to my house in twenty minutes and didn't even bother to check on the kids before I ran upstairs to change. I didn't have a lot of business attire, but a black skirt, white blouse, and sensible high heels went a long way. I put my hair up in a sloppy bun, added some non-prescription glasses to the mix, and I looked like Julissa Baker from south Florida. At least, that's what my ID said. I spent a grand total of ten minutes in my house and then I was back behind the wheel racing towards the prison. I shot Charles a text, because it would save the hassle of him having to take me back to his office if we just met at the prison. Thankfully, he agreed since I was already on the move. I got to Powhatan Correctional Center at five minutes past noon, but I still had to wait damn near a half an hour for Charles to pull up beside me.

"Took you long enough," I said, once he'd gotten out of the car.

"For the record, I'd like to say I think this is a bad idea."

"Duly noted, now look at this ID," I demanded, shoving my fake license in his face.

"Good quality, Ms. Baker. Let's get this over with before I change my mind," he said, leading the way across the parking lot

I held my breath as we went through the admission process, but I need not have worried, because Charles had written the book on the art of bullshitting. Ten minutes later, we were sequestered away in a windowless room waiting on my estranged husband to show up.

"Carmen, will you please stop pacing, you're making me nervous," Charles said.

I finally took a seat with my back facing the door and worked on controlling my heart rate. There was really no need to be nervous, I mean, it wasn't like I was about to come face-to-face with a complete stranger. It was only Zayvion. It was *only*

Zayvion. Still, when I heard the door suddenly open behind me, I got as nervous as a long tail cat in a room full of rocking chairs.

"This is a surprise and that usually means that something is wrong," Zay said from behind me.

"We need to talk," Charles replied.

"If it's about Carmen, I…"

I knew he hadn't finished his sentence because I was now looking him dead in the eyes.

"If it's about me, you what? Don't get lockjaw now, nigga, speak your mind," I encouraged.

"What the fuck are you doing here, Carmen?" he asked, clearly not happy to see me.

"I came to get some answers since you're obviously too much of a coward to pick up the phone and call a bitch. Take a seat, this won't take long," I replied, gesturing towards the chair across the table from me.

"This ain't a good idea, Carmen," Zay said, walking around the table and sitting down.

"But divorcing me is? You wanna leave the only bitch that's ever held you down, when it mattered the most?" I asked.

"Is that a serious question or did childbirth give you amnesia?" he asked.

"Look man, we've had our differences, but—"

"But nothing, bitch, I'm sitting in prison because of you! That ain't no goddamn difference, that's an act of war!" he growled through clenched teeth.

The fire in his eyes was something wondrous to behold, but for the first time ever, I was truly scared of this man and strangely, a little turned on by him too.

"It wasn't meant to be an act of war, Zay, it was meant to make you keep your promise to help Rocko," I said softly.

"So you chose your brother over your marriage, and I'm fine with that. Why are you here?" he asked again.

"Because I didn't choose my brother over my marriage. We can still make this work, we can—"

His abrupt laughter forced the rest of my words to die in my throat, and it made me want to leap across the table and punch him in his shit.

"I'm pouring my heart out to you and you think it's funny?" I asked, feeling my anger blood my veins.

"What heart, Carmen? Is that the same heart that justified taking me away from my kids? How's my son, by the way?"

"Which one?" I asked sarcastically.

I could tell by the look on his face that my jab had had the intended effect, but I knew it was counterproductive to my overall goal, so I didn't gloat.

"That's cute, *wife*. Just be sure you can explain all of this to them when the time comes," he replied.

"Zayvion, I know you, so I know you've got more lives than my alley cat. Do you really expect me to believe you haven't figured out a plan yet?" I asked.

"If he had I'd sure love to hear it," Charles chimed in.

"Maybe I do have a plan to get me out, but you wouldn't be happy if it was only me going free, would you?" Zay asked, looking at me with so much anger.

"He's my brother, Zayvion. What do you want me to say?" I asked, feeling more than a little helpless.

"I don't want you to say anything, sweetheart, but there may be something that you can do to save your brother," he replied, smiling devilishly.

"What?" I asked warily.

"You know what I like, baby."

"Okay, but you know I can't have sex this soon after giving birth. I'll come suck the skin off of your dick this weekend, I promise," I said sincerely.

"Nah, that don't work for me. I want some pussy right now," he replied, smiling wider.

It seemed like a lifetime ago when I'd had the thought that putting this good-good on him could change things for the better, and now that the opportunity had presented itself, I was shook!

"Right here, right now?" I asked, licking my suddenly dry lips.

"That's what I said, wife. What's it gonna be?"

After taking several deep breaths, I stood up and made my way to this side of the table.

"Now wait a minute, you two can't seriously—"

"Stop talking, Charles. It's your fault she's here in the first place. You can either watch us or watch the door so we don't get caught," Zay said, standing up.

When I attempted to walk into his arms, he spun me around fast and before I knew it, I was facedown and bent over the metal table. Thankfully, Charles was looking out of the tiny window in the door. Zay took his time lifting my skirt until it was bunched up around my hips, but then he tore my panties off savagely. It didn't matter to my body that it was too soon because my pussy was twitching wildly in anticipation.

"Open your mouth," Zay demanded.

When I did, he shoved my panties in my mouth while plowing his dick into me forcefully. With his first two strokes, I felt my stitches pop open, but I could tell he didn't care. He pulled my hair hard enough to bring tears to my eyes and he fucked me harder than I could ever remember him doing. My body was experiencing pleasure, but my heart was broken because I knew that there was no love in what he was doing. He was home fucking me. I let it happen though. I took his pounding blows even as the smell of my own blood filled my nostrils. For the first time in all my life, when my body rocked with orgasmic fulfillment, I cried silent tears that I couldn't explain. I could feel his dick throbbing inside me and I knew he was about to cum, but suddenly, he pulled out of me. I was bracing myself for him to ram his dick balls deep into my asshole without warning, but instead I felt the hot droplets of his cum smear all over my ass cheeks. To me, that was worse.

"Thanks for the ride, you were as good as I remember," he said, shaking my ass hard.

I couldn't even bring myself to look at him as I pulled my underwear out of my mouth and pulled my skirt down. I'd never felt more humiliated in my life, and it destroyed me that the man I loved the most that had done it.

"Oh, and I'll keep my word and get your brother out, but I still want a divorce. Charles, if yo pull some shit like this again I'm gonna have to find new representation."

Following that statement, Zayvion walked out of the room without a backwards glance.

"Carmen, are you-are you okay?" Charles asked.

"I'm fine, let's just go," I replied, discreetly using my panties to wipe up the blood flowing down my leg, before clutching them tightly in my hand.

We left the room and exited the prison without saying another word to each other, and I got straight in my truck and pulled off. Five minutes later, I had to pull over because I was crying too hard to see the road. I don't know how long I sat on the side of the road sobbing, but once I was able to get myself together, a new plan started to formulate in my mind. Instead of heading home, I decided to make a detour since I knew Iesha hadn't lived far from the prison. I arrived at my destination twenty minutes later, and after making myself presentable I got out of the car.

"Yes, ma'am, how can I help you?" an older white lady asked.

"I'd like to talk to the detective working the Iesha Barnes murder."

"One moment," she said, picking up the phone.

A few minutes later, a stocky black guy in a too-small gray suit came from behind the desk and stopped next to me.

"I'm Detective Morning, how can I help you?" he asked.

"My name is Carmen Miller, and my husband is Zayvion Miller. Soon to be ex-husband. I have information I think will help, but I need to know if I should tell you now or after the divorce is final," I said.

"How about you come with me and we talk in hypotheticals for the time being. Does that sound good, Mrs. Miller?"

"Perfect."

Chapter 9

Rocko

Two weeks later

"Wait a minute, you all ain't done. You missed that stack of papers over there," I said, pointing out a stack of request forms to the two C.O.'s searching my cell.

Of course, they ignored me and walked out, but I'd taken great pleasure in harassing them for the last twenty minutes, while they searched for drugs and weapons. They'd claimed the shakedown was random, but since this was the second time this week, it was obvious that someone was sending them at me and my celly. For that reason, I was determined to make sure the cops did their job and touched everything in my cell.

"It's shit like this that makes me want to beat them bitches again," Pittsburgh said, frustrated.

The bitches in question were none other than the infamous Kersee and Slim that we'd smashed not long after I got here.

"You know they ain't worth that, but I do think it's a good idea to get them out of the pod," I replied.

"You got a plan?"

"I've been working on a little something, but I've been trying to take my time with Shelby because she can be reckless," I replied.

"She gets that from her mom! It's like they think these are normal relationships that are acceptable."

"They just open, and it's our fault," I said, smiling ruefully.

"Yeah, well I've been on Bea's ass to not make my relationship with her so obvious, but she thinks that because she has seniority over the medical department, she can do what she wants."

"I'll try to get Shelby to talk to her if you want," I offered.

"Probably still won't do no good."

"Just yourself. Let's straighten up before they call us to dinner," I said, picking my clothes up off the floor.

Within ten minutes, we had the cell back in order, which gave me just enough time to holla at a man about my plan. When that was done, I made sure to put some oil on so I'd smell good for Shelby, and I posted up by the door to wait on chow call. Even though it was nice having Shelby to do whatever for me, I still missed Abby in a major way. I talked to her all the time and even talked to my daughter when she held the phone against her stomach, but it wasn't enough. It was killing me not to put her on my visitation list, but we agreed to wait and see what Zayvion would do, just in case she had to come work here. I hated waiting on that nigga, but Carmen swore on her kids that she'd gotten verbal commitment from Zay about getting me out of this mess. Despite everything that had happened, I knew my sister still loved her husband, but I didn't. Killing him was my first order of business, and to make sure that plan became reality, I was carefully grooming young Shelby. True to her word, she'd managed to get me a complete layout of this prison, and its identical twin that was located across the street. She also brought me a map of where we were in Waverly, Virginia. I knew that I couldn't take the chance of getting caught with any of that material, so she kept it stashed for me and pulled it out when I came to visit. She was extremely gullible, and this evening's mission was to find out how far she'd go for me. When the front door suddenly slid open, there was somewhat of a stampede as mufuckas made their way out, but I waited on Pittsburgh before merging with the sea of bodies.

"I'll be in and out," I said, once we got downstairs and outside.

"Yeah, I bet you will, but you better be careful because she's not taking birth control."

"How the fuck do you know that?" I asked, looking at him sideways.

"Because she talked to her mom about how beautiful mixed babies are and her mom asked the right questions."

This was the exact type of complication I didn't need, but I knew just how to use this info to my advantage.

"I appreciate the warning," I said, before separating from the pack and going to the door leading to medical.

Once I flashed my badge that proclaimed me to be an insulin-dependent diabetic, I was buzzed through the outer door. Of course I wasn't a diabetic, but fucking a nurse came with perks. I made my way quickly down the hall and was immediately buzzed into medical, where I found Shelby standing by the desk waiting on me.

"Right this way, Mr. Vargas," she said, smiling mischievously.

I followed her into a room and as soon as the door closed, I pulled her into my arms.

"I've missed you, baby," she said, kissing me with hunger and need.

I picked her up and sat her on the table, making sure to kiss her with the same passion, even though my mind was all business.

"I missed you too," I replied, when I was finally able to separate our mouths.

"Then why aren't you inside me already?"

"Because we need to have an important conversation," I replied, chuckling.

"We can do both," she insisted, wiggling her pants over her hips, revealing that she had no panties on.

"Sweetheart, it's not that I don't want to, but we really need to talk."

"So talk," she said, pulling my dick out and pulling me in between her legs.

The fact that I liked her aggressiveness was evident by how hard I was, and I showed her by diving deep with my first stroke. Our mouths melted back together, allowing me to swallow her sounds of passion while feeding off the taste of her desire. Her pussy was so hot and wet that it was intoxicating and for a moment, I lost myself in the depths of her ocean.

"B-baby, we have to t-talk," I said, slowing down my strokes, but not stopping.

"T-talk then," she panted, locking her legs around me and pulling me completely inside her.

"I need your h-help," I stammered, willing my eyes not to roll out of focus as her pussy somehow got wetter.

"Any-anything you want or n-need. I promise, oh God, I promise," she moaned passionately.

"Help me escape."

As soon as I whispered the words, I stopped moving so I could gauge her reaction.

"Why did you stop?" she asked, clearly frustrated.

"Did you hear what I said?"

"Yes, baby. I heard you, now come on," she replied, squeezing my ass cheeks.

"Wait, what's your response?" I asked.

"I kinda figured we were heading down that path. I mean, at least I hoped we were, because then that would mean you'd want a future with me."

"Of course I want a future with you, Shelby, how could I not? You've got me falling for you, and thinking about how cute our mixed babies would be," I said, kissing her lips gently.

"Really, Rocko? Are you sure?"

In response, I started moving inside her again with just the right amount of force to make her gasp with each stroke.

"I'll do-do anything for you, Rocko, I sw-swear," she professed sincerely.

I knew I had her, but I still fucked her like she was the only girl in the world for me. I made her cum twice before I came and then, it was time to get down to business.

"Where's the phone?" I asked, sitting on the stool in front of her.

She hopped off the table, pulled her pants up, and went to the cabinet under the sink. When she turned around, she passed me the cell phone I'd had her sneak in a week ago. I really wanted to keep it in the pod with me, but there was too much heat. Plus, we had to walk through metal detectors every time we came in or went out of the building. It made conducting business harder, but not impossible.

"I'll go get the Saboxin strips," she said, checking to make sure she looked ok before opening the door and stepping out.

When the door closed, I quickly turned the phone on and shot a text to Abby. She had no idea about Shelby and vice versa, so I had to always be careful about what I said. My text was simply meant to give her comfort by telling her that my backup plan was already in motion. I knew she was at work, which meant she wouldn't be hitting me back right away, so I told her I loved her before making sure to lock the phone so Shelby couldn't snoop. By the time she came back, I had it turned off and put back where she got it from.

"Here you go, babe, ninety strips," she said, handing me the small bundle wrapped in plastic.

Saboxin strips were about half the size of a normal band-aid and they were for people trying to kick their heroin addiction. In prison, they were a heroin junkie's dream though because they got you high, if you could afford them. The going price was a hundred and fifty a strip, but I was out to take a mufucka's clientele so my strips would only cost a hundred dollars. That meant I had nine thousand in my hand right now and it hadn't cost me shit, because Shelby's friend had a prescription.

"Thanks, baby, I'll be bringing you either cash money or green dots daily," I said, pocketing the work.

"What do you want me to do with the money?"

"Spend some, save some," I replied.

"I don't want to spend your money. I know you can take care of me, but I want to take care of you," she said, sitting in my lap and putting her arms around my neck.

"Who am I to argue with that?" I asked, pulling her towards me for a kiss.

We spent a few minutes fooling around before I had to leave so I wouldn't cause suspicion. By the time I got back to the pod,

Pittsburgh was already knee deep in a spade game, but he moved towards the cell when he saw me coming.

"In and out, huh?" he said sarcastically.

"Shut up, smart ass, it wasn't my idea."

"Right, right, right, well at least tell me you got what you went for," he said, pulling our door open.

The doors were run from the guard's tower, but putting a washcloth in the way kept the door rigged for easy in and out access. Once we'd slid in the cell, Pittsburgh kept a lookout while I peeled off ten strips.

"Get your popcorn ready," I said, handing him two strips.

"What are you talking about?"

"You'll see," I replied cryptically.

Being that I was the new kid on the block, I only had a few people that I was dealing with, but that was okay because slow money was sure money. Once I'd served my paying customers, I went and hollered at the white boy Toon, who was running Four Trey Gangsta Crip for the whole compound. I slapped him five and passed him three strips before nonchalantly walking away. With all business settled for the day, I decided to make one more move before lockdown. I hurried to the cell and grabbed another strip, and then I ran to the liquor man's house to do a little bartering. I was just making my way back down the stairs when all hell broke loose. I couldn't see clearly what was going on, but it was cartoon comical. There was a dust storm of feet, arms, and elbows, and screams could be heard. The deafening sound of the shotgun going off suddenly caused everyone involved to move around, unless they wanted to get hit by a real shot and not the warning. At the bottom of the pile lay Kersee and Slim, beat the fuck up. They didn't even try to get up, choosing to lay there until help arrived. It was a long twenty seconds later and by then, I was moving towards my cell. When I got to the cell, Pittsburgh stuck his head out and looked above.

"What happened?" he asked.

"I told you to get your popcorn."

"You should've told me exactly what was going on, you know I wanted to see that," he said, disappointed.

"More than you wanted to snort the dope I just gave you?"

"Touché," he replied, stepping out of the way so I could enter the cell.

The demonstration that had just taken place guaranteed there would be no more rec for today, but I was okay with that because there would be no more Kersee or Slim either. Fair exchange was never robbery. After the C.O.'s left and everything calmed down, I kicked back in front of Pittsburgh's TV with my soda bottle full of good whiskey, and sipped. The day could've been better, but it also could've been worse, so it was in my best interest to see the glass as half full. By the time I'd drunk half of the whiskey, I was nice and tight, and feeling better than any man serving a life sentence should. I was just about to suggest to Pittsburgh that we make something to eat when the intercom in our cell clicked on and froze us both in place.

"Vargas?"

"Yeah?" I replied cautiously.

"You've got an attorney visit."

Before I could say another word, the speaker clicked off and the door slid open.

"Attorney visit," I said.

"This late?" Pittsburgh asked.

We both exchanged a look because it was about shift change, and lawyers normally didn't come out this late. I quickly put the cap on my liquor, slipped my shoes back on, and passed Pittsburgh the rest of my Saboxin strips.

"If something goes wrong, just wait for instructions," I said.

"I got you."

I put some toothpaste on my tongue and headed out the door. When I got to the front door, I was met by a C.O. who handed me a pass and then he led the way downstairs. My eyes were wide open, looking for somebody to approach me and accuse me of putting a hit on the two mufuckas that just got smashed, but that never happened. I was escorted to the attorney visitation area and left there. A couple minutes later, a nicely put-together black woman entered the room. She stood about five foot seven, had chocolate skin that looked kissably soft, and weighed about a hundred and sixty pounds that contained curves her tailored suit could hide. She was beautiful, but by the look on her face, I could tell it was all business.

"Mr. Vargas, my name is Jasmeen Neale," she said, extending her hand.

She came with a firm grip and direct eye contact so it would be clear she was to be taken seriously.

"It's nice to meet you, Ms. Neale, but uh, what's this about?"

"Your sister, Carmen, hired me to try and get you out," she replied simply.

"Get me out? How?" I asked.

"I have some ideas, but it starts with the fact that she's gonna testify that her husband actually murdered the cop you were accused of killing."

"She can't testify to that, they're married," I said.

"They're married, but not for long. Divorce proceedings are underway."

Chapter 10

Zay

"I appreciate you making the trip, my nigga," I said, sitting down across the table from Shmurda.

"I wanted to look you in your eyes and see if you're full of shit, before I did something that can't be undone."

"Thank you. I know you loved Iesha, but you know I loved her too. I would've never done her like that, bruh, and I put that on my son," I said sincerely.

"So, who did it then?"

"The same nigga that tried to put me in the trick bag last time. He had some help from some unlikely people, but he was absolutely the brains behind the play," I replied.

"And where is he now?"

"In prison, but he won't be for long because I'm about to help him escape," I said, looking around to make sure no one was eavesdropping.

"If he did this on his own, killed Iesha and set you up, then why would you help him?"

"Because he's my gift to you. I'm gonna handle the other parties involved, but Rocko is yours. If you want him."

"What's the catch?" Shmurda asked.

"No catch, all you gotta do is be at the right place at the right time and he will appear like snow on Christmas morning."

"When and where?" he asked.

"I'll let you know, and I'll even throw in some cash because you'll be doing my partners a favor."

"I don't need cash because this ain't business, it's all the way personal," he stated coldly.

The murder in his eyes was easy to see, but it gave me warmth instead of chills.

"Listen, I got another visit so I ain't gonna keep you too long. I'll be in touch though," I said.

"About the visit I had to pay your wife…"

"What about it?" I asked, maintaining a neutral expression despite this being my first time hearing about a visit.

"I'm not sure what she told you, but I never threatened her or your kids. I only said my homies would move on you if shit didn't start making sense in a hurry."

"I get it, bruh, we good," I said, standing up to embrace him.

In the back of my mind I was fuming though because once again Carmen was displaying her treachery. Had I not had the good sense to call Shmurda, I never would've seen the knives coming! I don't know how I hadn't seen it sooner, but that bitch really wasn't shit! Once Shmurda left, I reclaimed my seat and waited on my next visitor to be shown in. Thankfully, I didn't have to wait long.

"You just can't stay out of trouble, can you?" she asked, giving me a much-needed hug.

"Is that your way of saying that you miss me, Doctor Silver?"

"To say I miss you might be putting a little too much on it, but I do miss the dick," she replied, laughing.

"Of course, you do!" I said, grabbing a handful of her thick ass and kissing her thoroughly.

When I pulled back, I could see the lust and longing in her eyes to match her previous statement, but we both knew she wasn't here for all that.

"How are the kids?" I asked, pulling out a chair for her to sit next to me.

"Bad as hell! Shit, my oldest son is gonna be sitting in here with you in a minute. Oh my God, your son looks just like you, even more so than Xavier did when he was born! Did Carmen tell you that she had the baby in my office?"

"We ain't speaking," I replied shortly.

"What? Why? Boy, she just had your baby, prematurely I might add, so you need to—"

"We ain't speaking because she's the reason I'm in here right now," I said.

"No what now? You're lying."

I could easily read the disbelief on her face, so I decided to tell her a little story that happened to be true. Five minutes later, I reached over and physically closed her mouth for her.

"So maybe you weren't lying but damn, that's dirty!" Dara said, shaking her head.

"You're right, but when you do dirt you get dirt. You can see why I need your help though, right?"

"What do you need me to do, sweetie?" she asked.

"You're my alibi, but I know how bad that's gonna make you look, and it could hurt your business. Plus there's a chance that the jury may not believe you, which means you put your business out there for nothing."

"First of all, I don't give a damn what anyone has to say or what they think. I'm a grown ass woman and I like dick, and if there are women on the jury, I'll let them know its good dick too. As for them not believing me...Well, I don't think that's a problem," she said, blushing.

"I've never seen you go red in the face. It's making me kinda nervous."

"Okay, so I have to tell you something, but I don't want you to get mad at me."

"Okay," I replied hesitantly.

"I've got cameras in my house...and they've recorded us having sex. No one watches the playback except me. It helps me to cum when I can watch you beat the pussy up. You film well, by the way."

I'd heard stories about people having those "eureka" or light-bulb moments, but I actually heard the switch flip with mine.

"You're a fucking genius!" I said excitedly.

"Glad you realize it. Oh, and they're date and time stamped too. So you see, you have what they call an ironclad alibi."

"In more ways than one," I mumbled.

"So, what's our next move?"

"Well, the first thing I need you to do is get all that footage to my lawyer so he can have it authenticated," I replied.

"You do remember the freaky shit we did, right?"

"Dara, do you really think I care if the world sees me licking your asshole? Girl, please, we're talking about my freedom! They can run the tape on CNN for all I care," I said seriously.

"Just checking. I'll get the tapes to your lawyer today if you want, but when do you go to court?"

"I'm not gonna wait until then, I'm gonna have him go to the district attorney and make a backroom deal in order for them to save face. Don't worry, I'll be out shortly," I replied.

"Good! Look, I know you got plans, but I get the dick first. Agreed?" she asked, extending her pinky.

"Agreed."

With the important business out of the way and brighter days ahead, we enjoyed the rest of our afternoon together. I told her I'd hit her up in a few hours after I talked to my lawyer, then I kissed her and smacked her on the ass as she walked away. It felt like I was walking on clouds as I made my way back upstairs, because I was positive I would have the last laugh, and Carmen wouldn't see it coming. Maybe if she was nice, I wouldn't throw her to the wolves. As I was walking past medical, I heard familiar laughter and when I didn't spot a C.O. at the desk, I decided to make a detour. I followed the sounds of carefree fun to the last exam room on the right, where I found Abby and Alexis kickin' it.

"Damn, I can hear your loud ass in the hallway. What are you two talking about?" I asked.

"Nothing," Abby replied quickly.

"With the twinkle in her eyes and the redness of your face, I'd say you all were talking about sex," I said, smiling.

Alexis laughed again and Abby's face got even redder, which told me all I needed to know.

"Fill me in," I said, stepping into the room and closing the door.

"She's horny, babe, that's what pregnancy does," Alexis said.

"Babe?" Abby questioned.

"Pregnant," I said.

Alexis's head was on a swivel looking back and forth between us two, but I was focused on sweet, not so innocent Abby.

"I'm assuming its Rocko's," I stated calmly.

"Of course. How long have you two been a thing?" Abby asked.

"That's a long story, but it has similarities to yours and Rocko's. I saved Zay's life when he got stabbed here," Alexis explained.

"You were stabbed?" Abby asked, her tone somewhat fascinated.

"Your man didn't tell you about the hit he put on me?" I asked.

"He wouldn't do that," Abby said quickly.

"Wait, Rocko did that?" Alexis asked, looking at me.

"He did," I replied shortly.

Suddenly, the harmless fun was a thing of the past as darkness swirled through the tiny room.

"That's water under the bridge though. Tell me, Abby, how horny are you?" I asked.

This question made Alexis burst out laughing, and Abby's face went beat red again.

"L-look at her shoes, babe," Alexis said breathlessly.

I looked down to see her sparkling white Adidas shell toes, but I still wasn't seeing the punch line.

"Okay," I said, slowly looking back up at Abby.

"Babe, she washes them twice a day so she can sit on the washer and dryer," Alexis said, laughing harder.

"Thanks a lot, Alexis," Abby said, pushing her.

"It's nothing to be embarrassed about, Abby, it's a known fact that all pregnant women get super horny. Maybe you should invest in some toys," I suggested.

"I don't do that sort of thing," Abby said quickly.

"What do you do, besides laundry I mean?" I asked, smiling.

She fought her smile for as long as she could and then she threw a middle finger up at me and Alexis. We all laughed, but I pulled Alexis to me and whispered something in her ear.

"You sure?" she asked, looking up at me.

"Yeah, baby, go ahead," I replied.

She gave me a slow, soft kiss before walking over to Abby and taking her glasses off.

"Wh-what are you doing?" Abby asked shyly.

"I'm doing what my man told me to do," Alexis whispered sensually.

Abby's eyes were full of uncertainty, but as Alexis started kissing a path across her collarbone and up the side of her neck, I saw excitement dancing in the flames of that uncertainty.

"It's okay," Alexis whispered, bringing their lips together for the first time.

Abby's whole body tensed up, but it didn't last long because in the blink of an eye she went from getting kissed to kissing back. I watched with hawk eyes as Alexis slid a hand inside Abby's pants, and I could tell the moment her fingers opened the door to her naughty secrets. The low moans coming from Abby's throat had the hair on the back of my neck standing up, along with a big part of my anatomy, but I remained a spectator to this sport. Abby was so caught up in the moment, I could tell she never felt Alexis work her pants and panties down her thighs and over her knees, but when Alexis stepped in between her legs Abby realized she was naked.

"W-wait, are we really doing this here?" Abby asked, clearly shocked by her own behavior.

"Shhh, just enjoy it," Alexis said, squatting down in front of her.

I could tell Abby was getting ready to put up a fight, but when she opened her mouth it stayed open, because Alexis was speaking to her in tongues.

"Oh God," Abby moaned, leaning back up against the wall and spreading her legs wider.

It was clear the fight to resist this temptation was officially over. At first, Abby had her eyes closed as she rode the waves of her forbidden pleasure, but suddenly she opened them and they locked on me. I knew my stare was intense enough to make her feel as though I was touching her, but I wanted more. With slow and deliberate actions, I reached inside my pants and pulled my dick out. To Abby's credit, she didn't immediately look at it, but as I began stroking it slowly, her eyes couldn't help looking it in the eye. The involuntary lip licking and unconscious eye bulge told me she liked what she saw, but I was more interested in knowing if she wanted it in her. I continued stroking it until my full potential was reached and then I stepped up behind Alexis. When she felt me pulling her pants and underwear down, she moved her ass to give me a better angle. I made sure I had Abby's undivided attention before I pushed my dick inside Alexis inch by inch. I set a slow pace so I wouldn't interrupt what they had going on, but I could tell Abby was just as quickly turned on by watching me fuck Alexis. We all moved together like synchronized swimmers, which allowed Abby and Alexis to cum within seconds of each other. Alexis's sounds of pleasure were muffled by her being face deep in Abby's pussy, but Abby had to literally bite on her fist to keep quiet. Right then, I knew it had been too long and she wouldn't be able to resist.

"You two should switch, and I'll just watch," I said, pulling my dick out of Alexis and backing up.

The look of uncertainty was back on Abby's face, but it didn't stop her from playing musical chairs. The way Abby looked at her clothes on the floor, I thought she might decide to get dressed, but she didn't. She and Alexis switched spots and Abby went facedown, like she'd lived in pussy her whole life. I could tell by Alexis's expressions that Abby knew what she was doing. And, I thought she should be rewarded for that. When I stepped up behind Abby, I knew she felt my presence, but she didn't stop what she was doing until I put a hand on each of her hips. Alexis and I locked eyes and I didn't see any disapproval from her, nor did Abby stand up or tell me to let her go. Still, I waited until she'd started licking Alexis again before I tested the waters by pushing the head of my dick inside her pussy. I immediately noticed how tight she was, but even more than that, I felt how her pussy walls grabbed at my dick like it was a life preserver. That was all the conformation that I needed, so I pushed all the way inside her.

"Oh God, no," she moaned softly.

"Do you want me to stop?" I asked, pulling out of her as slow as I could.

"I don't-I don't know," she replied.

I pushed inside her once more slowly, and then once with some power behind it.

"Abby, do you want me to stop?" I asked again.

Her response was to dive head first back onto Alexis, which allowed me to give her the dick she so desperately needed. I managed to hold out so Alexis could come twice and Abby came three times, and then I fucked her like she was my girl. By the time I came in her, she had a puddle dripping down her leg and into her sock.

"You feel better?" I asked, pulling my dick out of her and stepping back.

Abby didn't look at me or say a word. She just put her clothes on. I gave Alexis a nod so she would know I wanted a minute alone with Abby and with no hesitation, she got dressed and stepped out of the room.

"Abby," I said gently.

"He'll, he'll never forgive me," she mumbled, fighting the sob trying to rip from her throat.

"He'll never know, at least not from me or Alexis. This wasn't about him, it was about you."

"You expect me to believe you didn't get some sick pleasure out of fucking your enemy's woman? Or better yet, that I was too weak and pathetic to tell you no?" she asked bitterly.

That question told me her shame wasn't in what happened, but in the fact that she wanted it to happen. I crossed the room to her and turned her around to face me.

"Abby, look me in the eyes and hear what I'm saying. This had nothing to do with Rocko. You're a beautiful, intelligent and kind woman, isn't that enough of a reason for me to want to be with you physically?"

"I just don't want anything to fuck up my relationship with Rocko, because I love him," she replied emotionally.

"I'll never tell him, Abby, besides I'm sure he's doing the same thing."

"What are you talking about?" she asked.

"It's easier to get a nurse than it is a C.O. Think about it, a C.O. comes to work for the purpose of providing security for a paycheck, versus medical staff who are engrained with the empathy it takes to help people. Which person is more likely to care about a good man in a bad situation?"

I could tell by the look in her eyes that I was making sense to her, so I kept going.

"He's been there a couple weeks now, right? Sussex One is max security, which means it's harder to get shit like cell phones, but I'm willing to bet that had already called you from one."

"That doesn't mean he's fucking another female," she replied.

"You're right. Does he text more than talk? Has he sent you any pictures? Have you had phone sex yet?"

"There could be a number of reasons—"

"Or there could be one. His chick is holding the phone and he can only use it around her. You don't have to speculate though, because the nursing community is pretty tight for those of you that work in prison. Just ask Alexis to find out the truth for you. In the meantime, you need to understand nothing we did in here was about Rocko," I said, gently taking her face in my hands.

I was just about to lean in and kiss her when the door opens and Alexis came back in.

"The C.O. is back out there and I know you ain't got a pass, so it's time for me to escort you out," Alexis said.

I gave Abby a soft kiss on the forehead before letting her go.

"I'll go distract whoever it is," Abby offered, stepping away from me and heading out the door.

"So, are you gonna tell me what that was all about?" Alexis asked.

"Are you referring to the fucking or the mind fucking?"

"I understand both of those things, but I was referring to the intimacy. I don't like it," she replied seriously.

"I apologize," I said, pulling her into my arms and kissing her.

"Thank you. Now go take a shower, because I don't want you smelling like no other bitch's pussy."

I kissed her one more time before letting her go. She led the way out of the room and made sure I made it out of medical without any hassles. Once I made it back to my floor, I went straight to the phone to call Charles with the good news.

"I'm glad I caught you, Charles, I've got—"

"You've got a lot of trouble," he said, interrupting me.

"What are you talking about?" I asked slowly.

"Carmen has been talking to the cops, and you know why that's bad."

"Tell me everything, Charles."

Chapter 11

Carmen

Six days later

"Ariel, bring me a diaper for your brother!" I yelled.

"What brother?" she yelled back

I knew Xavier didn't yet understand any of what was being said, but he flashed his toothless smile all the same, forcing me to shake my head and chuckle.

"They both wear the same size, sweetie!" I yelled.

There was no immediate response, but I could hear her moving around upstairs, and then I heard her barreling down the steps louder than a jet at takeoff.

"Here you go, Mommy. Eew, Xavier, you stink!" she declared, slapping a hand over her mouth dramatically.

Again, he flashed his toothless grin as he kicked his little legs. Sometimes, it amazed me how I could feel love for this little boy considering his conception, and the growing hate I had for his father. I loved Xavier though and I treated him no different than I did Zay-Zay, Ariel, or RJ. Despite the hardships of being a single mother, these kids were where I found my joy and my motivation to go on. I'd thought that further hurting Zayvion by going to the cops would make me feel better after suffering through being treated like a common whore, but it hadn't. I still cried myself to sleep night after night, living through the pain of having everything once upon a time and now feeling like I had nothing left except my kids. I didn't just take joy in their unconditional love and innocence, but also in the fact that Zayvion wouldn't have the pleasure of seeing them grow up. I knew he probably thought he would, even if he was on the run, but the police now knew about his escape plan so he wouldn't get far. He might even die while trying to escape, and I didn't know if I'd feel bad about it. Hell hath no fury.

"I put Zay-Zay down for his nap and RJ is at the table with a coloring book. I can finish changing Xavier while you go take your bath," Karseea said, coming into the living room.

"Have I told you that you're a life saver? A God-sent angel!" I replied genuinely.

I'd known Karseea since she was a teenager working at her parents' Mediterranean restaurant in D.C., but we'd gotten closer since she'd moved in to help me with the kids full-time. She was a gorgeous twenty-year-old, but instead of living that wild life, she spent her nights at home with me covered in baby shit and vomit. I loved her for that.

"You may have mentioned it a time or two, but I can't take all the credit when you pay me like you do," Karseea replied, accepting the diaper from my hand and sliding into my spot on the couch. The mention of money made me cringe a little, because I knew I had to spend responsibly from now on. The quarter of a million I had stashed away wouldn't last long if I wasn't careful.

"I'll order the pizza too, so go enjoy your bath," Karseea said.

I headed for the stairs with the intention of doing exactly as she suggested. No matter how good modern medicine was, childbirth was still hell on the body, and I hadn't fully recovered. My pride wouldn't let me go to Dara after Zayvion had destroyed my stitches, so I'd gone to the emergency room and gotten sewn up, and I was still sore down there. Mentally, physically and emotionally, I was beat the fuck up and that's why I required one bath a day to soak the pain away. Once I got to my room, I filled the tub with my favorite bath gel and then I turned the Jacuzzi jets on. After quickly getting naked, I submerged myself in the hot water, exhaling like I was Whitney Houston and Angela Bassett. With my eyes closed, I just let my mind drift, focusing on happier times and more carefree days. It seemed like it took no time at all for my skin to get all wrinkly, but I'd faintly heard the front door open, which meant I'd been soaking at least thirty minutes because the pizza was here. I promised myself just five more minutes, but that became fifteen minutes. With great reluctance, I climbed out of the tub and walked into my bedroom naked in search of a towel.

"You always looked best wearing nothing at all," he said softly.

I stopped dead in my tracks, my eyes immediately going to the closed bedroom door where Zayvion was leaning against it, with a piece of pizza in one hand and his pistol in the other.

"Noooo," I said slowly, shaking my head and hoping I was imagining this whole thing.

"Damn, babe, that's all you have to say after all this time? You're normally a lot more talkative, or is that only when you're giving information to the police?" he asked, taking a bite of his pizza.

I could feel moisture dripping down the crack of my ass, but I didn't know if it was water or sweat. A bitch was most definitely nervous though!

"What are you talking about?" I asked, sounding a lot calmer than I felt.

"What am I talking about? Oh, so you think that because you haven't made an official statement that I still couldn't find out about you telling my dirty little secrets? Come on, sweetheart, I pay a lot of people a lot of money to be my eyes and ears in the darkest corners of the world. I'm just curious as to why though? Why do you keep testing me?"

It seemed like the more he spoke the bigger the Glock .40 in his hand got, and I couldn't keep my eyes from darting to it in anticipation of having to look down the barrel.

"You said fuck me, so was I not supposed to say the same to you?" I asked.

"Baby, if you wanna fuck, the bed is right there and I'll even put my gun away," he replied, tucking the pistol in the waist of his jeans.

I had no illusions about how fast he could make it reappear, but I did breathe a little easier for a moment.

"After what you did to me, you think I'd willingly lay down with you?" I asked.

"What I did to you? That's funny, considering that every time I turn around, you're trying to get me a life sentence or get me killed."

"You already killed me!" I yelled, suddenly losing the fight with my emotions and hating the tears now cascading down my face.

"I didn't do shit—"

"Own your truth, nigga! You took my brother from me and had the nerve to get another bitch pregnant! You treated me like I was some random hoe that you didn't owe shit, but I'm your wife, Zayvion. Your wife!" I said loudly.

I didn't remember having a conscious thought to move towards him, but somehow we were only a few feet apart and he hadn't moved.

"A wife gets her husband sent to prison? A wife tries in every way to paint a bullseye on my back? Well, if that's what being a wife is, then I'm glad our divorce will be final soon. Don't get it twisted though, Carmen, I can own my truths. Yeah, I got Iesha pregnant, and there's no excuse for that betrayal. I truly apologize for hurting you like that. As for your brother, this is a dog-eat-dog world and I've gotta think like a predator in order to ensure my survival. You may not believe it, but I lived my life like that so you and our daughter would never have to be without me. You think I'm the devil because I had the foresight to see Rocko's betrayal coming? Just keep in mind I never would've come at him if he didn't try to bury me first."

"So that makes it acceptable? That means I should be okay with what you did to my brother?" I asked sarcastically.

"No, that means you should've taken the time to really think it through. You set this in motion because you'd lost your brother but in the end, Carmen, who will you have? Once Rocko is out, he can't stay in the county. Who do you have, Carmen? Was it worth it?" he asked softly.

His words were like a knife to the heart and they caused me physical pain, but I wouldn't show it. Not to him.

"I have my kids, Zayvion. Can you say the same?" I contested.

"Actually, I can," he replied simply, smiling while finishing his pizza.

"You're on the run now just like Rocko will be, so—"

"What makes you think I'm on the run, sweetheart?" he asked.

"How else would you be out?"

"Why don't you call Detective Morning of the Richmond P.D. and ask him. I'll wait," he replied, crossing his arms over his chest and leaning against the door.

His confidence was giving me the chills and not in a good way. I could tell by the look in his eyes that I didn't need to call the detective because Zayvion wasn't bluffing. Somehow, the son of a bitch was once again a free man.

"How?" I asked simply.

"Let's just say I had an alibi, and we'll leave it at that."

"Of course you did, you sneaky motherfucker," I replied, shaking my head in disgust.

"Careful, sweetheart, you sound bitter and nothing in this world is worse than a bitter black woman."

"Yeah, except for a nothing-ass nigga," I said, smiling.

We stood there staring at each other for a minute, communicating so much without words because we knew each other that well.

"So, if you're not here to kill me or fuck me, what do you want, Zayvion?" I asked.

"Ah, so sex is back on the table? No pun intended."

"I'm glad you still think it was funny to humiliate me like that."

"Actually, I don't. It was something I had to reflect on because shit looks different in the daylight of freedom versus the darkness of incarceration," he replied seriously.

"Was that an apology?" I asked sarcastically.

His sudden movement caused me to freeze like a deer in headlights. I had no intention of letting him touch me, but when he pulled me to him and put his lips on mine, I melted. I don't want to kiss him back, but my tongue was doing all the work without me telegraphing a command, and my throbbing pussy was just as eager to join the show.

"*That* was an apology," he said, stepping back and releasing me.

I could feel my soul wanting to reach out to his, but deep down, I knew we were beyond that.

"You still didn't tell me what you're doing here," I said, grabbing my towel off the bed to busy my hands and cover myself, so I didn't feel so vulnerable.

"I came to give you this," he replied, pulling his gun back out.

For a split second, he had it pointed at my stomach and his finger was on the trigger, but he lowered it and extended it to me, handle first.

"I don't-I don't understand," I said, more than a little confused.

"I didn't think it was safe for you to be in this house without a way to protect you and the kids. I mean, you never know what could happen, right? Plus, I know you don't have that other pistol of mine."

The way he smiled when he said that made me want to smack him with his own damn gun, but I decided to keep it cute.

"That's thoughtful of you," I replied through clenched teeth.

"I'm glad you see that, because I'm not done. I also came to pick up Xavier."

"Excuse me?" I asked, feeling my face heat up with anger.

"My son, Xavier, I came to get him. Don't misunderstand me, I appreciate the incredible job you did, but the fact still remains that you killed his mom. It would be sick of me to allow you to raise him now that I'm out," he said logically.

There were so many thoughts, feelings and words running through my mind, I thought I would pass out from sheer information overload! By the skin of my teeth, I was able to keep it together.

"Me, kill Iesha? That's crazy, Zayvion. It almost sounds like you're wearing a wire and trying to entrap me."

This statement made him chuckle, but he did pull his shirt all the way up and then dropped his pants. We both knew when I looked at his dick I wasn't checking for a wire, but I managed to keep a straight face.

"Trust me when I tell you I would never need to entrap you, because I can prove real easy you killed Iesha. That's a conversation for another day though. I didn't come here to fight with you about Xavier, but we both know I hold all the cards legally when it comes to parental rights and custody," he said, fixing his clothes.

"So, you're gonna make the kids suffer to somehow spite me? Ariel loves her two little brothers, and RJ treats them like they're his little brothers too. I thought the kids were supposed to be innocent in all of this Zayvion."

I could tell by the flash of anger in his eyes that my statement struck a nerve, but I didn't care because I was only speaking the truth.

"I'll wait for you downstairs," he said, abruptly ending the conversation.

Even after he'd left the room, I still stood there staring at the door. I didn't know if I was hoping he'd come back or if I was afraid he would. After several deep breaths, I tossed the gun on my bed and went in my closet in search of clothes. Once I was dressed, I grabbed my cell phone off my nightstand, pulled up the detective's contact info, and called him. It couldn't hurt to be sure. Thankfully, he picked up on the second ring.

"Detective Morning, this is Carmen Miller and—"

"Mrs. Miller, I'm not allowed to speak with you, I'm sorry," he said, hanging up immediately.

I didn't get a question out, but his response told me everything I needed to know.

"Slippery mufucka," I said, under my breath.

Obviously, there was nothing left for me to do except deal with it. After stashing the gun under my mattress, I put on my resting bitch face and made my way downstairs. As I expected, Ariel was curled up in her daddy's lap, smiling from ear to ear, more happy than I'd seen her in a very long time. What I hadn't expected to find was my doctor sitting on my couch beside them, bouncing Xavier on her knee. When I looked at Karseea, I could tell she was extremely uncomfortable and unsure of what to do.

"Doctor Silver, I didn't know you made house calls," I said, stepping into the living room.

"Hey, Carmen," she replied nervously, looking sideways at Zayvion.

"I asked her to come look at Xavier before I took him with me, just in case you tried to accuse me of child abuse later," Zayvion said.

"You think it's okay to involve her in our situation?" I asked, noticing how close this bitch was sitting next to the man I was still technically married to.

"I'm not in your situation, Carmen, I'm only here because Zay asked me to be," Dara said.

"Bitch, I know this ain't what I think it is," I replied, becoming more heated by the minute.

"Not in front of the kids, Carmen," Karseea cautioned.

When I saw Ariel's expression had changed to one of quiet reserve, I reeled my crazy back in.

"Nah, this ain't what you think it is, but Zay is a friend," Dara replied boldly.

Right about now, I was wishing for the gun I'd foolishly left upstairs.

"Listen, Carmen, you seem all kinds of stressed so why not let me take Ariel for the night too?" Zay suggested.

"Yeah! I'm going with Daddy!" Ariel yelled, hopping out of his lap and spinning towards her room.

"You don't really think I'ma let you take my child, do you?" I asked in disbelief.

"You just got done preaching to me about the kids being innocent in all this, right? Well, you already know she's gonna want to spend time with me, and doing it this way will save an awkward conversation and her crying. Plus, you really do look like you could use a minute to yourself," Zay replied.

"So, you think taking our daughter to a hotel is gonna stop her from asking why *we're* not tougher, or why RJ and Zay-Zay aren't with you?" I asked.

"I think I can keep her occupied enough tonight to avoid all of those questions," he replied.

There was a lot not being said, and right now Dara's face was pissing me off, because I felt like she knew more than me.

"You know this ain't gonna end how you think it is, right?" I asked, addressing Dara.

"I'm sure I don't know what you mean," Dara replied, smiling.

"Hold on, I'll show you," I said, turning on my heels and running back upstairs. I quickly grabbed the gun from under the mattress and headed right back down to my living room.

"Carmen, she's not worth it," Karseea said.

"Karseea, go upstairs and help Ariel pack an overnight bag. Don't come back down until I tell you to," I instructed calmly.

Karseea immediately did as she was told, leaving only me, Zayvion, Xavier, and Dara.

"So, are you his new bitch or were you fucking him before our marriage went to shit," I asked.

"Does it matter?" she retorted.

The bitch had balls, I'd give her that.

"Dara, put Xavier down please," I said politely.

"Carmen," Zay said.

"I'm not talking to you right now, Zayvion, I'm talking to the hoe that was bold enough to come into my house and be nonchalant about having your dick on her breath. Now, for the last time, will you please set my stepson down," I said again, chambering a round into the gun.

"Hold him for a second, baby, I'm about to step outside and teach your ex-wife some manners," Dara said, handing Xavier to his father.

As soon as the baby cleared her hands, I raised the gun and pulled the trigger. The expression on Dara's face was complete shock, but it only lasted for a split second before the hole I'd put between her eyes started oozing and she collapsed on the couch. The roar of the gun had startled Xavier and made him cry, but Zay was rocking him soothingly, even though he never took his eyes off of me.

"Next time, leave your bitch at home if she ain't properly trained, because I don't got time to play. Now, get your kids and get the fuck out of my house before I silence you too."

Chapter 12

Rocko

Two days later

"You seem distracted."

"Huh?" I replied, looking up from the phone in my hand.

"You seem distracted," Shelby repeated.

She was right, I absolutely was distracted because Abby's texts as of late hadn't been normal. I couldn't put my finger on exactly what it was, but it seemed like something was on her mind. I'd noticed it during our phone calls, but I'd thought it was simply her missing me, especially because of how disappointed she'd been when I didn't send her a picture. Now, I wasn't positive that it wasn't more though.

"I'm sorry, sweetheart, I'm just trying to figure some shit out," I said, smiling at her.

"Anything I can help with?"

"No, I'd tell you if there was. You know how much I value your opinion and insight," I lied.

"Yeah...I've been thinking though, and I need to ask you something," she said hesitantly.

"Okay, what's up?"

"Are you-are you getting bored with me?" she asked.

I could see her heart swimming in her big green eyes, and I knew all the insecurities that were pulling her under water, so I chose my words carefully.

"Come here," I said, putting the phone aside, and opening my arms so she could sit on my lap.

Once she was seated, I turned her face to me so I could look her in the eyes.

"Shelby, do you know why I love you? It's not because of what you do for me or because the sex is phenomenal, it's because you're an amazing woman. At your age, most girls are worried about superficial shit, but you're on your grown woman shit, and that speaks to your maturity. What I'm saying is, you're the type of woman a man builds his life around, not the kind we get bored with. Are you bored with me?" I asked.

"No, no, of course not! I'm falling in love with you, but I'm scared because I don't want to be in this alone."

"You're not alone, baby," I whispered, pulling her towards me, and kissing her tenderly.

Even as our tongues quenched each other's thirst my mind still went back to Abby. My sweet Abby. I didn't want her worried or stressed, but I knew that was damn near impossible, with the future being as uncertain as it was. The money I'd been sending didn't provide the security she wanted, and the only thing that would was my freedom. That meant one of the plays had to work.

"Are we good?" I asked, pulling back so I could look up into her eyes.

"Better than good, babe, I love you so much," she replied, smiling wide enough for me to see all thirty-two of her teeth.

My response was to kiss her again quickly.

"So, what were you able to find out?" I asked.

"Well, no one had ever broken out of this prison, but three have tried though. Two of them are currently serving twenty-year sentences in long-term segregation at Red Onion State Prison, and the third one got killed during his attempted escape,"

The facts she laid out weren't at all comforting, because it sounded like a mufucka was gonna have to be Rambo to get out, and I wasn't no damn John Rambo.

"So, basically it's impossible," I said.

"No, I didn't say that. I think there's a way, but it would mean I'd have to be on the run with you."

"Okay, and?" I asked impatiently.

"If we called for an ambulance to take you to the hospital, we could make a run for it. My mom knows a lot of people at the local hospital, so if we stage it to look like I overpowered the driver and took off with you, then we'll get away."

"What about the transport van with the armed guards in it that accompanies the ambulance to the hospital?" I asked.

"Well, since I'll know who the driver of the ambulance is, I figured I could have a few guns on board. I know how to shoot and I'd bust my gun for you," she declared, using her best hood chick impersonation.

Her idea sounded wild as hell, but it just might be crazy enough to work.

"Do you have the right kinda guns for what you're suggesting?" I asked.

"What kind would we need? I mean, my dad has a lot of guns."

"Babe, we're talking full automatic firepower, pull the trigger and bullets fly on repeat. I'm talking about machine guns," I replied seriously.

"My dad has one that sits on a tripod and the bullets come on a belt that you feed into the gun. Would that work?"

"Yeah, I'd say that would work," I replied, surprised and impressed.

"Good, so all you have to do is tell me when you want me to put our plan in motion."

"How about we save that as a last resort and see how these other situations play out?" I suggested.

"If you say so, but I personally can't wait to have you out so I can get this when I want it," she said, reaching in my pants and massaging my dick tenderly.

"Don't start nothing we can't finish."

"You already know how magical my mouth and kitty are, I can finish you in minutes," she bragged, smiling.

"What about your ass? You still ain't let me sample that big old juicy thing."

"That's because you haven't asked. You should know by now that if you wanted to put your dick in my ear so I could hear you cumming, I'd let you. My body is yours, Rocko, all yours," she replied seductively.

I really didn't intend to fuck her today, but she was talking that talk I liked. The sudden vibration of my phone put a halt to the seduction though. When I looked at it, I saw a text from Carmen, telling me to call her from this phone when I could.

"Aww shit," I mumbled.

"What's wrong, babe?"

"I don't know, but I gotta make a call," I replied, gently pushing her off my lap.

"I'll go warm your food up while you do that," she said, leaving the room.

I quickly dialed Carmen's number and waited for her to answer.

"What's wrong?" I asked immediately.

"Bruh."

Just that one word and her tone told me shit was real.

"What is it, Carmen?" I asked.

"I did something stupid."

"Okay. That doesn't surprise me a whole lot, knowing you, you probably went and visited Zay," I said.

"Nah, it's worse than that, but I can't really say it so I need you to follow me on this."

"Okay," I replied slowly.

"Wait, let's start with the bad news first. My plan to get you out ain't gonna work."

"What are you taking about, that lawyer you hired was on point. I know she can get me back in court," I said confidently.

"It's not gonna work because Zayvion is out," she replied, sounding more than a little frustrated.

"Wait, if he's out, then that means—"

"No it don't, because the nigga is out legally," she said.

"There ain't no way that's possible, Carmen, tell me you're bullshittin'."

"Oh I wish I was, and it's more than possible because the nigga had an alibi," she replied.

"For three fucking days? Hell nah, I ain't about to believe no shit like that," I said, shaking my head.

"Bruh, I tried to call the detective on the case and the nigga straight up told me he couldn't talk to me anymore."

"Yo, that's crazy! He might've flipped on the connect, because I don't think—"

"Nah, it ain't that because he's out handling business right now, plus he wouldn't put the kids in danger," she stated.

This shit was truly mind-blowing, but if this was the bad news, I knew I was gonna hate whatever comes next.

"The fact that you knew his move means you two are...what?" I asked.

"It ain't even like that, but that brings me to my next point. So he comes by the house to pick up Xavier, but he doesn't come alone. You already know that shit got sideways from there, and I did the one thing you ain't never supposed to do in front of anybody. And, I did it in front of Zay."

I didn't respond right away, but instead tried to process what she was telling me. There were a couple different scenarios I was entertaining, but the one I kept coming back to was the one I was praying she wasn't talking about.

"No, Carmen, tell me you didn't—"

"Yeah, I did," she replied softly.

"Oh, God...dammit! So what did he do?"

"He made me take all the kids and leave the house, and by the time I came back everything was straight. That was two days ago, and he's been here since, but we ain't doing shit except cohabitating," she replied.

Aside from my son, Carmen was my favorite person in the world, but right now I literally had nothing nice to say to her. Of all the mufuckas to kill somebody in front of, she picked the one nigga we'd both turned into an enemy! The one nigga that would love to destroy her world! I didn't put it past that sneaky bastard to bring a bitch around Carmen, just because he knew how she'd react. Shelby's sudden return forced me to abandon the investigative questions I was about to fire at my sister's simple ass.

"You know this is crazy, right?" I asked calmly.

"Yeah, I know, but there's nothing I can do about it now."

"So, what's next?" I asked, accepting the bowl containing pot roast and mashed potatoes Shelby offered.

"Believe it or not, he told me to tell you to be ready because the curtain is going up soon."

"Really?" I asked, completely shocked.

"Yeah, we just had this conversation before he left a little while ago. I don't know any of the details, but I know he's gonna keep his word,"

As good as the food smelled, it was temporarily forgotten while I envisioned my freedom. Despite Zay finding a way around the set-up, I was still gonna accomplish the main objective, and that was all that mattered.

"Carmen, I want you to listen to me. If that nigga wants waffles from scratch with a side of head at three a.m., you better stretch your jaws and fire up that stove, you hear me? Do what you gotta do for me please and I'll owe you for life," I vowed seriously.

"I got you, bruh, you already know that. Do you want me to let Abby know what's going on?"

"Yeah, do that for me because good news is definitely needed," I replied, looking at Shelby to make sure she couldn't overhear Carmen.

"I'll do that now, you just maintain in there and I'll see you soon. I love you."

"I love you too, and make sure you tell RJ I love him," I said.

"I will."

When I hung up the phone, I did so with more hope than I'd had in a long time. I didn't know what Carmen had done to convince this nigga to get me out, but I was grateful and to demonstrate that, I was gonna kill Zay ASAP. Then she and I would truly be free.

"Is everything alright?" Shelby asked, looking at the untouched food in my hand.

After turning the phone off, I passed it to her so I could pick up my fork and dig in.

"Mmm, this food is amazing! And as far as everything else, let's just say that you might not have to become a fugitive in order to be with me," I said, smiling.

"Does that mean one of your other plans is working?" she asked, hopeful.

"It looks that way, babe."

"That's perfect, that means you'll be out by the time the baby is born," she said excitedly.

It took me a few moments to realize that she couldn't be talking about my baby with Abby, because she didn't know Abby, and that could only mean... "Baby? What baby?" I asked, looking at her closely over the bowl I had lowering by my mouth.

"Our baby! Well it's not official, because I'm only like four days late, but my period is always on time, so I think I'm pregnant," she replied with that same excitement.

The only two words I could think of were *oh fuck*, but I knew that wasn't the right thing to say in this moment.

"Well, babe, if you're now eating for two why are you letting me hog all the food?" I asked, pushing the bowl towards her.

This made her laugh, but she did take a piece of the tender meat and put it in her mouth.

"My mom is the best cook in the world, but don't worry, she's promised to teach me so I'll make a good wife for you. You should've seen us making this meal least night because she had some of her nurse friends over that work at other prisons, and we were all in the kitchen cooking and talking about the men in our lives. It's so crazy that my mom and I are pregnant at the same time because now—"

"Wait, whoa, slow down. Did you say Bea is pregnant? Is your dad the dad?" I asked.

"Nope, he got his nuts clipped awhile back, plus they don't have sex anymore. My mom got tired of him getting his nut and then leaving her in bed with a vibrator to finish herself off, so that's why she's with Pittsburgh. She says Pittsburgh fucks her like she's young and she loves it."

"That's more than I needed to know. Does Pittsburgh know that he's about to be a daddy?" I asked.

"I'm not sure, but she won't be able to hide it forever."

Despite the good food I was enjoying, I still couldn't wait to get back to the pos and see the look on my celly's face when I gave him the shock of his life. Knowing him, he'd been fucking Bea, figuring the batteries were dead in her uterus!

"Do you want a boy or a girl?" Shelby suddenly asked.

"As long as our baby is healthy, I don't care."

"I want a boy, a little you, and we can name him Rocko III," she said, wishfully.

I could see stars in her eyes, but it was clear that she didn't see the panic in mine. In the clink of an eye, I made the rest of my food disappear before handing her the bowl.

"Next time I come over here, we're gonna try for twins," I said, kissing her.

"Or we could try now. You don't have to go yet."

"If we don't want things to be obvious, then I do, but I promise this sneaking around shit will be over soon," I replied, kissing her briefly again.

"Will you call me tonight?" she asked.

"Don't I always?"

"I love you, Rocko."

"I love you too, baby," I said, kissing her stomach.

I left the room casually, but I really wanted to sprint because this bitch was more clingy than new Velcro! I knew it was my own fault, and it would have to remain a necessary evil until I was a free man. It could be worse though, I could be like so many of the dudes in prison who had nothing and no one. I kept that in mind as I got my pass from the nurse's desk and made my way back to the pod. I figured that after I had a good laugh at Pittsburgh's expense, we'd eat and then smoke a little green, but as soon as I got to the top of the stairs and saw Kersee by the ice machine, I knew my plans were about to change.

"One on one bitch, bring it," he said, pulling out a six-inch ice pick.

The smart move was probably to run, but I was dumb and I go dumb hard, so I stepped into the ring with him. The way he moved signaled that he had some experience, but I still had the reach advantage. I wasted no time popping my jab and putting a little blood on his teeth. My next jab caught him in the nose, but I got greedy and tried to punish him on an overhand right. That mistake got me stuck in the hand with his ice pick. I could tell he saw it as a victory, while I saw it as motivation. I went at him again with the same two-punch combo, but I pulled a lot off of the right hand, so when he swung the ice pick I could stop my forward momentum. The result was he missed, and that gave me a chance to grab his arm. I don't know which excited me more—the sound of his arm breaking, or the screaming that came from the pain.

"Oh nah, bitch, don't holla now," I said, tossing him up against a wall.

I finally stopped throwing punches and he fell face-first on the floor. He probably thought I'd spare him like last time, but I'd learned my lesson about showing a nigga mercy. I grabbed his ice pick in one hand and his leg in the other and then dragged him in the stairway out of the camera's sight.

"Since you're the bitch, I guess I should fuck you," I said, turning him over on his face and pulling his pants down around his ankles.

Without any hesitation or second thought, I spread his ass cheeks with one hand and rammed the ice pick in his asshole with the other. His screams now had a girlish quality that made me smile, but I knew better than to stay and savor my victory. I walked calmly out of the stairway and went to the front door of my pod. I was holding my breath until the C.O. buzzed me in, but even after I was in the pod I could only exhale slightly because I knew my time was limited. Luckily, no one was out for rec and I was expected to go straight to my cell, so me suddenly jogging to my room didn't seem too weird. The door was open before I got there and it shut as soon as I got to the room.

"Who you running from?" Pittsburgh asked jokingly.

His smile froze on his face the moment he saw blood on my hands.

"What happened?" he asked, hopping out of bed.

"That's a long story. Right now, I need you to get my strips out of the stash, and count ten out."

While he did that, I quickly washed my hands and cleaned my wound. The thing I loved about Pittsburgh was that I didn't have to tell him common sense shit. Not only had he peeled the ten Saboxin strips off, but he'd re-wrapped the rest using latex glove fingers, in case I had to hide them in my ass or in my mouth. No sooner had he passed me the bundle, our door opened behind me.

"Vargas, the captain wants to talk to you about you shoving a knife in another inmate's asshole," the C.O. said.

"I ain't got nothing to say," I replied, popping the strips in my mouth, and putting my hands behind my back.

The feel of cold steel on my wrists didn't affect me like it normally would, because I knew it was almost over. I was almost free.

Chapter 13

Zay

"Thanks for coming over," she said, holding the door open so I could pass her into her apartment.

"I gotta admit, it's my curiosity that brought me this far," I replied, admiring the effort she'd put into making this rental her home.

"Well, my plan was to just talk to you when I went to work, but imagine my surprise to find out you'd been released."

"Surprise or shock? You're forgetting I do remember how scared you were that first night you came to see me, Abby," I said, taking a seat on her couch.

"I wasn't scared...okay, so maybe I was a little scared," she conceded, blushing almost as hard as she had the last time I'd seen her.

Thinking about when that was had me looking at her in her oversized sweatshirt and leggings a little differently. I knew what secrets those clothes were hiding.

"Your fear was understandable. I mean, you probably only heard horrible things about me, and you trusted the source."

"Yeah, I *did*," she replied.

Her emphasis on the past tense didn't escape my attention, but I chose to let that go for now.

"I'm sure there was some truth to what Rocko told you about me."

"Well based on what I've seen, you're not the deal, although I'm sure you're capable of bad things," she said.

"Oh, I'm more than capable."

"Can I ask something? I mean, you don't have to answer if you don't want to," she said nervously.

"Whether or not I'll answer all depends on what you ask."

"Did you...Did Rocko really kill that cop?" she asked.

This definitely wasn't the question I was expecting, so I took my time trying to figure out why she was asking it, before I decided whether or not to answer. The nervous energy she was putting off didn't seem like the undercover-sting-action type, but I still took my time, slowly looking around the room to see if anything struck me as odd.

"No," I replied simply.

"Oh. Why did you tell me the truth?"

"Because that's what you needed. That's why you asked. You're trying to figure out if you can trust me," I stated, matter-of-factly.

"Can I trust you?"

"You should only trust yourself," I advised.

"That doesn't answer my question."

"Then maybe you're asking the wrong question. Why do you want to trust me?" I asked.

"I don't know, because you're different, you're so different than what I'd thought you'd be."

"And Rocko's not, because he lied to you like every other man before," I concluded.

Her quick eye aversion told me I'd hit the nail on the head, but I wasn't surprised because I knew the nigga she loved better than she did.

"You were right about everything. I even had dinner with the bitch last night."

"I take no pleasure in being right. I only told you the truth because I didn't want to see you beat yourself up over some misplaced guilt," I said

"And that's the thing, you cared and you didn't have to. That's rare in this world."

"I care because I feel like you're a sweet girl who accidentally stepped into a situation where you could easily become collateral damage if you're not careful. This ain't your world, sweetheart, and I don't feel good about you falling victim to it," I replied.

"This isn't Alexis's world, but you don't try to stop her from living in it."

"You can't help who you love," I said.

"So you love her?"

"I have love for her, but she's in love with me," I replied honestly.

"Yeah, I kinda got that feeling when I asked how to contact you."

"I'm actually surprised she gave you my number," I admitted.

"Oh, she only did it under one condition. I had to promise not to kiss you."

Hearing this made me chuckle, because it sounded exactly like some shit Alexis would say.

"You wanna let me in on the inside joke?" She asked.

"It's nothing, really. She just didn't want me to be intimate with anyone except her."

"Does she not remember what happened in that room? I mean, it does not get much more intimate than that, you made me..."

"I made you, what?" I asked when she stopped talking.

"Cum."

With her speaking that one word, we both knew it was now clear why she'd called me to come over.

"Take your clothes off," I said.

"I'm fat."

"Take your clothes off," I repeated slowly.

She hesitated for a few more seconds and then she pulled her sweatshirt over her head, revealing her firm breasts and slight baby bump. Next came the leggings, and of course there were no panties covering her cleanly shaven pussy. I took my time drinking in her beauty from head to toe, loving how her whole body blushed under my scrutiny.

"You're beautiful," I said.

"No, I'm—"

"You're beautiful," I repeated, looking her squarely in the eyes.

When she smiled, I got up and come around the coffee table to stand in front of her.

"Now take my clothes off," I demanded.

The fear in her eyes was real, but she was starting to understand she was gonna have to take what she wanted. The shaking in her hands was noticeable, but she managed to get my t-shirt up and over my head. When it came to my jeans, she didn't bother with the button, choosing instead to simply pull them down to my ankles. She hadn't anticipated my boxers going with my jeans, but suddenly she was eye level with a monster.

"I-I'm not sure I can take all of that in my mouth," she shyly.

"I never said you had to try, sweetheart."

"But what if I want to?" she asked, looking up at me in a way that made my dick jump involuntarily.

She didn't wait for me to say a word before she started sucking on the head of my dick like a Jolly Rancher. I was trying to play it cool, but the more of me she took in her mouth the harder it became to breathe. I thought when she gagged she'd stop, but she simply readjusted, relaxed her throat muscles, and tried again.

"My God that's sexy," I said, putting my hands straight up in the air to resist the temptation to grab her head and fuck her face.

Once she got used to all I had to give, she began bobbing, moving at the pace of a see-saw. Watching her devour me was beyond erotic, it was majestic and magical. You would think she was new to this because of how slow she was moving, but her speed allowed her to be thorough, and the force of her suction was tornado strong.

"I-I'm not gonna last long if you keep this up," I warned.

"You're not leaving until I have you every way I want you," she replied, going right back to what she was doing.

I tried closing my eyes to stop seeing her, but the image of what she was doing was imprinted on the back of my eyelids. When she suddenly increased her speed, I gave in to the moment and grabbed a fistful of her hair. Just as I was about to cu she pulled my dick completely out of her mouth.

"My face!"

"Wh-where?" I asked, confused.

"Cum on my face," she said, before putting my dick back in her mouth.

At this point I didn't care where I came as long as it happened! It only took her ten seconds to make my knees rattle. I tightened my drip on her hair and pulled my dick from between her lips just as I reached the point of no return. Cum shot all over her lips and cheeks, making her eyes sparkle with excitement. I stroked my dick a few times to make sure she got all of me, and then I slapped it across her lips like it was a gerbil feeder, so she could suck out the last drops.

"D-damn," I said, admiring the freak in her.

"Oh, this is just the beginning," she replied, rubbing my cum all over her face and down her chest.

When she stood up I didn't know what to expect, but she took my hand and led me to her bedroom. When she pushed me down on the bed and climbed on top of me, I realized Pandora's Box was open, and there was no going back. I thought I would need at least ten to fifteen minutes' recovery time, but as soon as she slipped me inside her tight walls, I was all the way turnt up.

"You sure you know what you're doing?" I asked.

"Are you?" she countered coyly.

Until Abby, I'd never known anyone to go zero to one hundred on the dick, but one minute she was getting a feel for me being inside her and the next, she was riding me at a full gallop. I could've sworn she was possessed and the devil was chasing her, but I was not mad at all. After cumming twice on top of me, I rolled her on her back and taught her about good dick.

"My-my baby! Don't-don't hurt my-my baby!" she pleaded, as I bent her in half and dove inside her with the force of a jackhammer.

When she came again, I thought for sure that her neighbor would call the cops because she screamed so loud. Still, she hadn't had enough because she turned over on her stomach and demanded I fuck her in the ass. I was worried about her ability to take what I was giving, but I shouldn't have because her ass was so tight I came in five minutes. I'd thought life was pretty good as I laid there in her bed trying to catch my breath, and then the unthinkable happened. She started crying. As a black man that's consciously aware of the racial tension that still exists in this world today, I knew it was all-bad that this white woman was laying next to me crying after all we'd done. A huge part of me was ready to become one with the wind, but that would make me a bigger piece of shit.

"Come here," I said, pulling her into my arms and stroking her back gently.

"I-I'm sorry, it's not you, it's-it's—"

"You thought it would make you feel better and it didn't," I said.

My accurate assessment made her cry harder, but at least I knew this wasn't my fault.

"She's p-pregnant, and she was bragging about the f-future they're gonna h-have. The f-freaky sex!"

I was sure I was only getting bits and pieces of the story, but the big picture was becoming clear.

"Do you think he loves her or he's using her?" I asked.

"I don't know. It doesn't matter though, she's pregnant."

It matters because you have to decide what your next move is. We both know you deserve better, and I'm not just saying that because I'd like to make you mine. I'm saying that because you know what Rocko's life is about, and that ain't about to change once he's on the run. He'll have to use his wit, his charm and anything else to survive, and the fact that he's booking your heart ain't something he can factor in," I said honestly.

"So you're saying I should just give up?"

"No, I'm saying you need to love you and that baby more than anyone else," I replied.

She didn't immediately respond to what I said, but her tears dried up at heart. I continued holding her, but it was a battle to keep my mind off the fact that she was naked.

"You really are different," she said, looking up at me.

"I try to be."

I could tell what she was gonna do even before she made her move, but I was okay with it and that's why when she leaned towards me, I met her halfway. Our first kiss was soft and an exercise in getting to know each other better. It got deeper though and before I knew it, I was back on top of her, inside of her, making love to her instead of fucking. I took my time with her, but in the end we ended up on our sides spooning, both of us with a hand on her stomach as we found ecstasy. In my heart, I knew I wasn't shit for what I was doing, but I justified it with the knowledge that I'd set her free. After the sweat cooled on our bodies, we made it back to the living room and got dressed before she walked me to the door.

"If you call, I'll come," I said, kissing her one more time.

"I know," she replied, smiling.

By the time I got back to my car, my mind was focused on nothing but business. I called Shmurda to make sure he was on his way, and then I called my guy, Hector, to tell him I was on my way. I knew part of Abby had felt bad for using me, but I'd used her too and not just for sexual gratification. I shot Alexis a text message, telling her I needed all the info she had on the new bitch Rocko was fucking with, and then I got back on the road. My meet up with Hector took a few minutes, but it still took me two hours to get to Iesha's house. I hadn't been here since she'd been killed, and the pain of those ghosts wasn't something I was prepared to endure alone.

"Took you long enough," he said, as I got out of my car.

"Traffic bruh, traffic. I appreciate you meeting me down here though."

"It's cool, I get it. She was my favorite cousin," Shmurda replied genuinely.

I took a deep breath and then went to the front door. I wasn't sure what to expect, but I knew this couldn't be avoided forever. Opening the door brought a blast of stale air rushing out, but thankfully, not the smell of death. Ultimately it was anti-climactic when I walked into the house, but that was better than being overwhelmed by emotion.

"You check these out, I'll be right back," I said, passing him the packet of papers I'd picked up from Hector.

The first thing I noticed when I walked into the living room was that the couch was gone and sections of the carpet had been removed. I knew immediately that this was the room she'd died in and my steps faltered, but I managed to keep walking. My next obstacle came when I made it upstairs to the bedroom. All I could think was that if these walls could talk, they'd have a lot to say, and that made me smile despite the sadness I felt. I didn't waste any more time strolling down memory lane, instead I went to the closet to find what I knew would be there. Given that the scene that was staged downstairs had been so full of clues pointing at me I knew that cops hadn't thoroughly searched the house. From the way shit was looking, if they had searched then Carmen would have been in jail before the sun had set. Once I had what I needed I cleaned out Iesha's safe, putting the contents in an old shopping bag, and I headed back downstairs.

"Do I even want to know how you were able to get authentic paperwork for me to pull this shift off?" Shmurda asked when I made it back to the dining room.

"Let's just say my connect had a long reach and almost limitless power, not to mention, they're motivated to see this nigga disappear for God."

"Seems like it. All the papers are dated for two days from now," he said.

"Yeah, that's Friday, which means nobody will know anything is up until Monday at the earliest. All you gotta do is get you a nice suit and be ready."

"And, what are you gonna do?" he asked.

"I'm gonna make sure that anyone who cares about Rocko either forgets he existed, or they stop existing themselves. That way, by the time that shit hits the fan, nobody besides law enforcement will care where he is and everybody will think he's on the run."

"Where should I dump the body then?" he asked.

I'd contemplated this question in more than one occasion, but now that I was standing here, the answer finally clicked.

"Bury him in the backyard here, that would make Iesha smile," I replied.

"Yeah, it would."

I was about to suggest we kick back and smoke a blunt when my phone started going off. I pulled it out to find that Alexis had invited Shelby over, and that I should be there in an hour.

"That's the last loose end right there," I said.

"Aight, well you handle that while I put the rest of the plans in motion," he replied, putting the paperwork back in the manila envelope and standing up.

We embraced as men do, and then he left. I was just about to follow him out when a thought occurred to me, making me go back upstairs and take a quick shower. I kept clothes here for when I used to spend the night, so I threw on something fresh and then got on the road again. Twenty minutes later, I was at Alexis's house and just as I suspected, the first thing she wanted to do was talk about Abby. I told her everything she wanted to hear, and then I ate her pussy until she screamed like a banshee. By the time Shelby showed up, Alexis was all smiles. Shelby was young and bubbly, and so green that she didn't realize she'd stepped inside the lion's mouth. About an hour into her visit, Alexis made some excuse to leave the room for a minute, but what she was really doing was sneaking out of the house to establish herself a public alibi. Her text ten minutes later, signaled that it was now my turn to play host to our guest.

"So, Shelby, can I ask you a question?"

"Sure," she replied.

"How much did Rocko tell you about his escape plans?"

"Only that it'll be happening soon and—wait, how do you know about that?" she asked slowly.

I could tell by the look on her face she knew she'd said too much. She didn't yet realize the danger she was in though.

Chapter 14

Carmen

"Mommy, I want Daddy."

"Your dad will be back soon, Ariel. Eat your food," I said, putting the plate of fish sticks and French fries on the table in front of her.

Her response was to get her little arms over her chest and put on the stubborn face I was all too familiar with.

"Ariel, don't make me beat that ass today, now eat your food," I said again, leaving her and RJ at the dining room table together.

I loved my daughter, but my patience was thin these days, so my willingness to whoop ass was at an all-time high.

"Carmen, you know you're my girl, but you look like shit," Karseea said, when I walked into the living room and flopped down in the recliner.

"Who am I trying to impress?"

"Things still the same between you and Zayvion?" she asked.

The concern in her voice was touching, especially considering she knew I'd killed a bitch in this very room. We didn't talk about that though.

"You mean my soon to be ex-husband/roommate? Yeah, shit is still the same with the stubborn jackass," I replied.

"You need to make him remember what you two had once upon a time, because that shit was a ghetto fairy tale."

"You don't see the way he looks at me now. It's like he looks through me because he doesn't know who I am anymore, and he doesn't care," I said softly.

"So make him care! You've got something no other bitch on this street had, you've got history. You've got memories and experiences with this man and no amount of throat, pussy, or ass can change that, sis. If you want your man, then you're gonna have to fight for him, and nobody said it had to be a fair fight."

The wrinkle in her eyes made me laugh, which was something I hadn't done in a long time.

"I think you've been hanging around me too long because you sound downright diabolical," I said.

"I'm just saying, if you'll kill for a man, then you obviously love him because ain't no dick that good."

"It is though," I whispered.

"Mmm, is it?"

Her response had both of us laughing until tears were leaking from our eyes.

"I normally don't kiss and tell, but that man knows how to lay pipe," I admitted, thinking about the many, many occasions he'd torn up my foundation with his pipe laying.

"Damn, you make it sound like its magic or something."

"Woman to woman, I'ma keep it real with you. I've never really been mad at any woman who got hypnotized and then dickmatized. As my husband, Zay is supposed to keep it in his pants, but knowing how good it is, I've never been able to hold a bitch accountable for wanting more. Their only loyalty is to themselves, you understand? Now, when a bitch don't know her place, that's when I gotta remind her," I said.

"Wow, you make it sound…wow."

"Now see, that look on your face is why I don't kiss and tell, because I can see the curiosity all in your eyeballs," I said, half-jokingly.

"Nah, I mean you did just make his dick sound like the cure for cancer, but I know how dangerous it is. No thank you."

"Actually, it might not be a bad idea for us to have a three-some, you know just to spice shit up," I suggested.

"If that's how you feel then go for it, but my pussy will not be the third ring in that circus, no ma'am. Aside from the fact I love you like a sister, and I very much value my life, I've only slept with a handful of guys. Not even a full handful. My point is that ain't none of them had the dick you just described to me, and so my search for the Holy Grail doesn't need to begin and end with Zayvion. Thank you, but no thank you," she replied seriously.

"I was just testing you," I said, laughing at the look on her face.

"Yeah, well I pass all tests, but you've proven my point even more. Let's put this into perspective real quick. Outside of Zayvion fucking other women, would you say he's a good man and father?"

"Yeah," I replied without hesitation.

"Okay, and the bitch he got pregnant, this happened while he was locked up and she was bringing him shit in?"

"It sounds like you're making excuses for him," I said.

"No, I'm looking at it realistically. It wasn't like he was out and he made a choice to lay down with this woman and give her a child. Correct me if I'm wrong though, but don't didn't you tell me you told Zayvion you wanted another baby and then he got you pregnant?"

"While his other bitch was pregnant," I pointed out.

"My point is, that even in the midst of all that chaos he still was willing to give you what you wanted, and tie himself to you for an even longer time. Does that sound like a man that was ready to leave you for some convenient pussy?"

Her question didn't simply make sense, It brought revaluation with it that I hadn't seen until now. I'd been so hurt by what Zay had done to Rocko that another bitch being pregnant had caused me to become completely blinded by rage. Zayvion had made some catastrophically bad decisions, but we could've worked through it if I hadn't taken matters into my own hands.

"I hear what you're saying, Karseea, but honestly I think it might be too late," I said.

"If you give up, then yeah, it is too late. But we both know you've got too much fight in you to give your dude up to Becky with the good hair. You could've easily let him walk out of here with that white girl with the fat ass the other night, but you didn't. Now, I'm not saying that you need to necessarily go to that extreme again, but you get my point."

Our conversation was suddenly interrupted by the crying of a baby, causing Karseea to jump up and run for the stairs. Her words stayed with me though, swimming around my head and my heart almost like they were taunting me. Was it really as simple as to fight or not to fight in order to save my marriage? I didn't think so, I thought we were past that, but Karseea's words made too much sense to simply ignore. The love I had for Zayvion was undeniable, and part of me understood I had to go through the pain of losing him to realize what he still meant to me. I was tired of that pain though. I just wanted to love and be loved again. With this thought in mind, I picked up my phone off the table and sent Zay a text, asking when he'd be coming back. Not wanting to alert him to all that I was feeling, I quickly sent a follow-up saying Ariel was asking for him. It was like Karseea said. This didn't have to be a fair fight. While I waited on Zay's response, I decided to call Abby and check on her and the baby.

"Abigail, I haven't heard from you, are you okay?" I asked when she answered.

"H-hey, Carmen. I'm fine, I was just resting. Kinda had a long day."

"How's my niece, you ain't stressing her out, are you?" I asked.

"No, I'm actually feeling a lot less stressed then I have in recent memory. Great sex will do that for you though."

"Really? So I guess that means you've been to see my brother," I stated casually.

"N-no. When I said great sex, I meant I'd taken care of myself. I mean, who knows our bodies better than we do?"

I didn't know that I was buying her response, but I let it go because who she was fucking wasn't my business.

"Well, have you talked to Rocko?" I asked.

"No, not since he got put in the hole."

"The hole? For what?" I asked, immediately worried.

"His celly called me and said something about Rocko shoving a shank in a dude's asshole, but only because the dude came after him with it."

"When the fuck did this happen, and why didn't you call me?" I asked, upset.

"I got the call today, and I thought you already knew, since you and him are so close."

There was something about her tone I didn't like, but I took a few deep breaths before I responded.

"Abby, is there something on your mind, because if there is, I'd rather you just say it instead of being passive-aggressive."

"Did you know your brother got another nurse pregnant at the new prison he's at?" she asked pointedly.

"He what?" I asked, dumbfounded.

"You heard me Carmen."

"But he's only been there a couple weeks, how the fuck is that possible?" I asked, mystified.

"Obviously doesn't waste time."

"Listen, I don't know where you got that information, but I think somebody is just fucking with you—"

"I heard it straight from the bitch's mouth! She was only too eager to talk about how he'd ate her pussy and made her cum like no other man had. She even described his dick since she'd memorized every inch of it with her tongue and brain! And before you offer up some lame excuse whatever he's done. I know from my own experiences that men in those situations do some dumb shit, but it doesn't mean that he doesn't love you," I said.

"It may not mean that, but I'm learning to love me more."

"What does that mean exactly?" I asked.

"That means I lied to you earlier. I had a man fuck me today like I've never been fucked in my life. He fucked me in my ass, he came on my face, and he left me walking funny, but I loved every second of it. The part I loved the most though was that even after we'd done all of that he helped me to see my worth when the guilt started to set in. He helped me to understand that it was okay to love a man I couldn't have, but it wasn't okay to love one not worthy of me. Rocko had a choice to make, and he wasted no time making it. I hope that he can live with his because I'm living with mine."

The fact that she'd hung up the phone didn't make me pull it away from my war or change the fact that I was speechless. Utterly and completely speechless. The only thing I could really think was, good for her. I loved my brother, but he'd made his bed and now he had to lie in it. All I know was that I wasn't about to be the one to tell him that his baby mama was using another man's semen as a skin care product! I applauded Abby's independence, but I wasn't the messenger that was getting shot for nobody. My phone's sudden vibration in my hand had me looking at the screen where Zay's message had just come in.

"Ariel, are you done eating?" I hollered.

"Almost, Mommy."

"RJ, don't you eat her food for her," I warned.

"I'm not," he yelled.

"Karseea?" I called.

A few seconds later she appeared, carrying Zay-Zay, who was all smiles.

"I need a favor," I said.

"What's up?"

"Zayvion said he'll be here in a couple hours, so I need you to get all the kids out of the house for a while," I replied.

"That's my girl! I can do that for you, but you gotta help me get everybody ready."

We spent the next hour making bottles, changing diapers, getting the kids dressed, and making sure everybody had extra clothes. Karseea had to call for reinforcements, in the form of her fifteen-year-old sister Meeska since she decided that Chuck E. Cheese was their destination. I gave her the keys to my truck and five hundred dollars before kicking everybody out. Once the house was empty, I ordered some Chinese food and took a quick shower. I thought about getting all dressed up, but that seemed pointless when all I really wanted was to rekindle the flame between me and Zay. It served my purpose to simply have on my robe and nothing else. Once the food arrived I put it in the oven to keep warm while I set the table, and lit some candles. I lit candles in the living room too, and then I turned down all the lights. When I heard Zayvion's car pull up out front, I took my robe off and took a seat at the dining room table to wait.

"Daddy's home!" he called out, coming through the door.

"In here, daddy," I replied seductively.

Moments later, he walked into the room and my mouth went dry.

"Where are the kids?" he asked, taking in the scene in a fleeting glance.

"They're out. It's just us."

"Carmen, don't do this," he said, turning around to leave.

"Zay wait. I just wanna talk and have dinner, is that too much to ask?"

He stopped in his tracks and turned back towards me, but didn't speak at first.

"Dinner, Huh? Well, I smell Chinese, so I know you didn't cook," he said, taking a seat.

"I wouldn't dare try to cook Chinese, but I did order your favorite though," I replied, getting up and going to the kitchen.

I quickly put his sweet and sour chicken, along with his egg rolls, on one plate and took it out to him. Then I came back to fix my own plate of beef and broccoli. I could've made both plates at once, but I wanted him to see me naked as much as possible.

"Damn, I forgot the wine," I said, sitting my plate on the table and returning to the kitchen.

I could hear him chuckling under his breath, but he didn't say anything. I grabbed a bottle of red wine and two glasses before returning to the dining room.

"What are you laughing about?" I asked, moving to his side of the table and pouring him a glass of wine first.

"You and the games you're playing."

"Games?" I asked innocently.

"Yeah games, Carmen. You're wearing a helluva outfit for dinner and conversation."

"I'm glad you approve," I said, smiling and reclaiming my seat.

"Sex isn't our problem, plus I don't really think you want this evening to end in the bedroom."

"Why Zay, because you're gonna fuck me like last time?" I asked bitterly.

"I understand the way I went about that wasn't right, but if I recall correctly you did cum."

"So did you. In my ass like I was some slut you didn't wanna get pregnant on accident. Do you know how that made me feel, Zayvion?"

"About as it made me feel to know that you of all people had put me behind bars," he replied, his tone laced with anger and pain.

"Zay, I…I'm sorry. No matter how mad I got, I never should've taken it to that extreme or tried to get the cops involved after what happened in the lawyer visit. I'm not making any excuses, but hurt people do hurt people."

His immediate response was to pick up his fork and start eating his food, prompting me to follow his lead. The silence between us was uncomfortable, but I know I had to endure it if I actually wanted to have a meaningful conversation.

"Let me ask you a real question, Carmen. What is your apology supposed to mean to me?"

"It should mean I'm asking for your forgiveness. I'm asking that you give us another chance, because we've been through too much to throw it all away without a fight," I replied.

"So, you want to fight for your marriage? Now? Why not when you first found out about Iesha? Why did it take us going through everything we've been through, for you to realize we're worth fighting for? Didn't you know that if you would've given me another chance, I would've chosen you eleven out of ten times? Didn't you know I loved you to the very depths of my soul, Carmen?"

"Baby, I couldn't see any of that, I was just so devastated! I was destroyed and all I could think about doing was lashing out until you felt what I did," I replied, angrily wiping the tears from my eyes.

"I did feel what you felt. I felt it the day you walked into the interrogation room and revealed what you'd done. I never thought I could stop loving you, not for any reason."

"You don't, you don't love me?" I asked weakly.

"Honestly, I don't know anymore. I do feel sorry for you."

"I don't want your goddamn pity, Zayvion, I want you back!" I replied, fighting to control my anger.

"You know, you never asked me why I agreed to still get Rocko out."

"Okay," I said, thrown off by his abrupt change of topic.

"Because it's poetic justice. You traded out love and loyalty for a self-serving, lying, cheating piece of shit, and I'd bet this what you thought I was. You know what the difference is between your brother and me? He's a dog and I'm a wolf, and a wolf don't spare the sheep. So I'm gonna get your brother out, just so you can look at your life after that and ask yourself if it was worth it."

I sat there silently evaluating him, wondering if this had always been who he was or if I'd pushed him over the edge. It didn't really matter in the end because the cruelty of his intentions triggered something with in me.

"You're overlooking something, sweetheart," I said, taking a sip of wine.

"What's that?"

"I'm not a sheep. In fact, I'm as much wolf as you are, so I feel comfortable telling you that we will be together," I replied smiling.

"Or?"

"Or, I promise I'll kill you my damn self."

Aryanna

Chapter 15

Rocko

Two days later

On its best day, the hole was extremely boring, but somehow being in the hole at a max security prison only made it worse. At lower levels, you could find an officer who'd give you a book to read just to keep you quiet, and not throwing piss and shit and them. The C.O.'s at Sussex didn't give a fuck. They were only giving you what you were allowed to have. That list of items consisted of paper, a flexible pen, your legal work, your mattress, and a blanket. So far, I'd spent my first day reading over my case front to back, but I couldn't do that more than once without screaming in frustration. That meant I had a choice of either staying bored, or getting high, and it was an easy decision.

I'd seen Pittsburgh tear off a piece of a Saboxin strip and pit it on a spoon full of water until it dissolved, and then he'd snort it. I followed the same steps, and an hour later I was asking myself why the fuck I'd never rode this rollercoaster before! Admittedly it wasn't typical for a black dude to fuck with this kind of drug, but the country had integrated a long time ago so why should the white boys have all the fun? I don't know how much I snorted, but I know it was enough to hear solos, see sounds, and forget what the meaning of time was. I did know that it had been too long since I saw Shelby, and I missed her. I wanted to fuck her while I was this high because I could guarantee that if she wasn't pregnant now, she would be when I was done! She hadn't been at work though. I wanted to call her, but I couldn't use the phone until after I had my disciplinary hearing next week. So all I could really do was see exactly how high I could get, and that was a challenge I accepted.

"Vargas, rise and shine," a C.O. said, kicking my door and turning on the bright light. This had been a recurring theme by the officers. Some just for laughs, and others who wanted to thank me for literally putting a knife in dude's ass.

"How many bags do you need?" he asked.

"Huh?"

"Bags, to pack your shit. How many?" he asked slower.

This got my attention enough for me to get out of my bed and move on unsteady legs to the door.

"Two bags should be enough, but where am I going?" I asked.

"I don't know, but you're out of here," he replied, pushing the bags through my tray slot and walking away.

I wasn't about to ask any more questions, and since my dope was already stashed in my paperwork, I just started throwing shit into trash bags. Within a few minutes, I was packed up with my shoes on, ready to go, but of course I had to wait ten extra minutes because the motto in prison is hurry up and wait.

"Step to the slot and put your hands behind your back," the C.O. said.

I did as instructed and he handcuffed me. When the door slid open, there was a cart that my bags went in, and then we were on the move. I expected to be uncuffed once we were out of the segregated housing unit, but the C.O. just kept a firm grip on my elbow and escorted me across the yard. The big surprise came when we took the door to intake.

"Am I being transferred?" I asked.

"Yes, you are, you lucky devil."

I suddenly wasn't as excited as I had been moments ago, because this meant whatever plans Zay had made would be fucked, and I was losing Shelby in the process! This could not be happening again. When we finally made it to intake, there was a slim built, brown skin dude in a dark blue suit and red tie waiting on us.

"His property will be stored here until he gets back, I've already cleared it with your captain," the man said to the C.O.

"Fine by me. You got restraints?" the C.O. asked.

The man held up a pair of handcuffs on a waist chain, shackles, and the black box that went over the handcuffs. I wasn't even in the car yet and I was already hoping the ride was short because all of these accessories were uncomfortable. It only took a couple of minutes for him to have me hooked up like jumper cables, and then I was being led outside to the car.

"So, where am I going?" I asked.

When I didn't get a response, I looked at the man holding my elbow, but he simply looked back at me.

"Where am I going?" I repeated.

"For a ride, nigga, now shut up."

It was on the tip of my tongue to say some slick shit, but I ain't never seen a mufucka win a fight in handcuffs, so I kept my mouth shut. He shoved me into the backseat, got behind the wheel, and got us on the move. I thought I was trippin, but I could've sworn this cop car smelled like weed. No doubt it was the Saboxin that had me trippin' because the nigga driving was too uptight to be closing trees in his government-issued car. Since he wasn't about to tell me where we were going, I had no choice except to sit back and enjoy the ride on the wave of dope in my system. I had no idea how long I'd nodded out, but eventually, I realized that the car had come to a stop and nobody was in the driver seat. I looked out the window expecting to see some type of police station or jail, but all I saw was houses.

"I know this nigga didn't stop to make a booty call," I said aloud, looking around to see if I spotted him anywhere. I'd just made up my mind that I was gonna do everything to get this mufucka fired when I saw him come out the door of the house directly in front of me. Instead of getting back in the driver seat though, he came to my door and opened it.

"Get out," he demanded.

"Wh-what?"

"I said get your bitch ass out the car, nigga," he growled, grabbing me by my waist chain and pulling me out.

I hit the ground hard and at that moment, I stopped giving a fuck that I couldn't win a fight while wearing restraints.

"Bitch ass cop, I'ma have your job and your prison," I said, glaring up at him.

"Man, you should like a real hoe right now."

"Whatever nigga, you heard what the fuck I said. Un-em-ploy-ment," I taunted.

He pulled me to my feet and pushed me in the direction of the house he'd come out of. When I reached the doorstep the door swung open, and when I crossed the threshold, a pair of large hands grabbed me by my shirt.

"What the fuck—"

"Shut up bitch," a voice said, right before I was hit flush in the chin with a devastating punch.

I'd been in plenty of fights in my life, but I had never been hit that mufuckin' hard! My knees immediately gave out and as I was falling, I felt another blow to the back of my head that filled my vision with stars. I was still conscious as I was being dragged down the hallway, but I was lost as to what the fuck was really going on. I knew about police brutality, but these niggas were beating me like we was in the street and I owed them money. I was damn near ready to apologize for what I'd said outside, but then I heard something that made me understand that the worst was yet to come.

"Sit him in that chair," a familiar voice said.

I was immediately picked up and put in a hard wooden chair, and that's when I came face-to-face with the last man I wanted to see.

"Sup bruh?" Zayvion asked, smiling at me.

"When I said I wanted you to break me out, this wasn't what I had in mind," I slurred, trying to fight off the dazed feeling from the punches I'd taken.

"Yeah, I bet, but you know I'm full of surprises and I have a flair for the dramatic. I really hadn't planned on us ever sharing the same air again, but I wanted you to know just how real shit is. You see, in your twisted mind you think I'm the bad guy, because I had an insurance plan to protect myself from you. But in reality, that plan would've never been put into play if yo hadn't snitched. I'm not the bad guy, I'm the smart guy. You still thought you were smarter though, especially when you convinced Carmen to go along with your bullshit. You actually sent me a kite telling me

138

that good doc couldn't come between what you and her had, you remember that? Let me show you what good dick can do," he said, stepping in front of me and holding up his phone for me to see.

Even before he pressed play, I could see Shelby's face on the screen.

"Rocko, if you're watching this, I pray you don't get mad because I'm only doing this because I love you. I will always help you in any way I can and well, this is what he said I had to do in order to get you out."

When Shelby backed up, I could see Zay standing behind her, even though I couldn't see his face. I could definitely see that Shelby was naked though. When she bent over, I knew what was coming.

"You act like I loved her or something," I said, smirking.

"No, but you thought she loved you," he replied, laughing.

"Didn't you just hear what she said, nigga? Why she was doing this?" I asked.

"Yeah, but watch her," he replied.

As badly as I wanted to look away, I couldn't. I saw the surprise on her face when he first pushed inside her and then I watched her forget that she wasn't supposed to be enjoying herself. Her moans started off soft, but a minute later she was calling him daddy and throwing that ass back at him. Once she came the first time, she really started acting a fool, demanding that he fuck her harder and put it in her asshole too. I knew how easy it was for her to cum, but in the ten minutes he made me watch, she came no less than five times. Suddenly, he stopped fucking her and without having to be told, she quickly turned around and got on her knees. She ate the dick and sucked his balls, finally finishing up with hot cum all over her face.

"I-I think we should erase that one and start over, because I don't want him to think I enjoyed it," Shelby said, wiping the cum off her forehead and licking her fingers clean.

"Did you enjoy it?"

"Don't tell Rocko, but you're the best I ever had. Can I spend the night with you? Wait, why are you pointing that gun at me. I'm pregnant—"

She never got to finish her thought before her brains got pushed out.

"Oops," Zayvion said, laughing as he pulled his phone back.

"So what, the kid probably wasn't mine anyway," I said, nonchalautly.

"Oh, so if it was Abby, then that would make a difference? Hold on and let me see if I can find Abby's video," Zay said.

"Who you fooling, nigga, there ain't no way that my bitch would let you touch her, and if you raped her, I'll kill you," I vowed.

"Nah, it wasn't rape, but it was fun," he replied, turning its phone back towards me.

The shock of seeing Abby's face was too real for words.

"A sex tape? Zayvion, yo should know I've never made a sex tape," Abby said, blushing.

"Why not? You're beautiful, you're a freak, and you take direction very well."

"I am not a freak! Okay, so I'm only a freak with you, and I still don't know why that is," she replied.

"So, are you trying to tell me I'm the only man to cum on your face, fuck you in the ass, and have a threesome with you?"

"Yes, yes, and yes! I told you I'm just not like that, but you're—well, you already know what you are," she said, blushing again.

Hearing her admit to all the stuff she'd let him do had my stomach rolling, but I was determined not to give this mufucka the satisfaction of throwing up in front of him.

"I don't know what I am, Abby. What am I to you?" Zayvion asked slyly.

"You're special to me, and to my baby. I'm sorry, our baby. We're both lucky to have you."

"I won't make you keep watching this, Rocko. I mean, you get the point. I will tell you I shot that video last night and yes, I did fuck her righteously afterwards," Zayvion bragged, putting his phone away.

"Yo, you cold," the nigga in the blue suit said, laughing.

"You can't play mind games with me bitch-ass nigga, I know I'm the one that got Abby pregnant," I said.

"True, but who will your daughter call Daddy?" Zay asked.

I lunged at him, but I was immediately hit by another power punch from my blind side that put me on the floor.

"You're about to find out the meaning behind the saying, 'if you play pussy you get fucked,'" I heard Zayvion say.

All I could see was the shadow of a brown bear leaving over me, but I was determined to kick his ass if I ever got up.

"He's all your Shmurda, just send me the video," Zayvion said.

I could see him walking away and that only meant one thing. I was gonna die.

"Bolt his ass to the floor," the fake cop ordered.

Before I knew it, the bear had me up and he hit me with a vicious head butt that put me on the borderline of consciousness. I could feel the chain come from around my waist, but instead of coming completely off, I was forced to the ground on my face with my hands out in front of me over my head. The sound of power tools came in quick like a Nascar pit crew, and before I knew it, I was stuck to the floor like the carpet.

"Before we get started, let me introduce myself. My name is Shmurda, and Iesha was my favorite cousin. Now I know you're gonna say you didn't kill her, but it was your plan and so, like *The Godfather*, I'm here to settle all family business today. This nigga here that's been using you as a punching bag, well you can just call him daddy and you'll learn why soon. Are there any questions before we begin?"

"Fuck you niggas, I ain't afraid to die," I replied, accepting my fate.

"Oh, this is gonna be worse than death. Show him what's up," Shmurda said, taking a step back and pulling out his phone.

Suddenly the big bear of a man was standing in front of me, holding a police flashlight with both hands.

"You gonna beat me to death with that?" I asked sarcastically.

"In a manner of speaking, but maybe you should look closer before you crack jokes," Shmurda advised.

When I did a double take my mouth went dry because I saw it wasn't a flashlight. He was holding his greased-up dick and it was at least a foot long. I tried with all my might to pull my hands and legs free of the floor, but the bolts wouldn't budge. The men's laughter only made me panic more and struggle harder.

"Get him, bruh," Shmurda said.

"Don't fucking touch me!" I yelled, still fighting to get free.

The feeling of horror that came over me when the big dude moved out of my sight had me sweating instantly. I could feel the blood trickling down my wrists as the handcuffs bit into my skin from the struggle, but I didn't care. All that mattered was me getting off this damn floor.

"Get the fuck off me!" I screamed, when I felt my pants and boxers snatched down.

Feeling his massive weight on my legs brought the terror to life.

"Just kill me! Just kill me!" I yelled, squirming mightily.

I didn't know if they could hear me over their own laughter, but the moment I felt something probe in between my ass cheeks, I did the only thing I could do. I shit on myself.

"Ay bruh, he thinks shitting on himself will save him," Shmurda said, still laughing.

"Just more lubrication," came this deep voice from behind me.

I opened my mouth to beg for death again, but all I could do was scream as he drove his dick into my ass. I felt myself ripping and tearing, but all I could do was scream as he went deeper and deeper with each thrust. Finally, I vomited, but not even that stopped him. I was fucked.

Chapter 16

Zay

"I appreciate you seeing me without an appointment, Charles," I said, sitting down across the desk from my lawyer.

"It's not a problem, plus I like when we can meet in my office, instead of the other places I find you in. So, what can I do for you?"

"Well, Charles, you are a jack of all trades when it comes to this lawyer thing. I mean, it's really like one-stop shopping when I come to you. Today, I wanted to talk about my assets in the event of my death," I said.

"Okay, well let me get this on tape so my secretary can transcribe it later," he replied, pulling out a mini recorder.

"First off, if I die, the house I bought for Iesha is not to be sold for any reason. It goes to my son, Xavier, and you're in charge of paying the taxes on it until he's twenty-one years old. At that age, he can decide if he wants to keep it or sell it, but no one is to live in it in between now and Xavier's eighteenth birthday. If for some reason, Xavier should become emancipated by the courts and become a legal adult before he turns eighteen, then he can move into his mother's house. Now, when it comes to the rest of my assets and money, I want everything split up evenly between my kids, and held in a trust until they're eighteen. You will be the executor of that trust too, Charles."

"I appreciate the trust and confidence you're putting in me, Zayvion, but I have to ask. Why now? I mean, you've lived your life a certain way for a long time, but you've never made these preparations or gone to this extreme," he said.

"I've lived my life by seeing what's coming, as much as I can anyway. The most important lesson I've taken from this last situation is that the only person I can trust is me, and my kids are what matters the most, so I gotta make sure they're straight."

"What about Carmen?" He asked, hesitantly.

"As of right now, Carmen isn't my concern, but I'll let you know if that changes. Now, turn the tape recorder off," I ordered, pulling my phone out of my pocket.

"Is something wrong, Zay?"

"Nah, we just need to have a conversation that probably shouldn't be recorded. I want you to see something, Charles, and then we'll talk," I said, locating the video I wanted, and passing him my phone.

When he pressed play, I could tell by the way his expression changed from nonchalant to disbelief that he was shocked, but he didn't look away from what he was seeing. When he finished, he looked up at me with so many questions in his eyes.

"Wh-why didn't you tell me about this?" he asked, passing me my phone back.

"I honestly didn't think about it until Dara said something about filming us having sex. That was something that me and Iesha did a lot of, so much so that she'd put motion sensitive cameras in a few different rooms. Of course, there'd be no way for Carmen to know that."

"And so you've got her on tape torturing and killing Iesha," he said, mesmerized.

"I do."

"Okay, what's your plan?" he asked.

"Right now, this will serve as an insurance policy, and you will be the only person with a copy," I replied.

"Insurance against Carmen? You think Carmen is gonna make another move against you, or kill you?"

"I can tell by your tone that you still have no idea who my wife is, but that's okay. Honestly, I'm still finding out new things about her myself. Do you remember that old movie, *The Devil's Advocate*?" I asked.

"Vaguely."

"Okay, well to paraphrase, beware of the wolf in sheep's clothing," I stated.

"Jesus, you make Carmen sound evil."

"Do you wanna watch the video again?" I asked, extending my phone back to him.

"No thank you," he replied quickly.

I didn't insist, but I did shoot it to his work email so that if he ever had to use it, it would come from his legal business account.

"Aight, so I just sent you a copy. For now the way we'll do it is if you don't hear from me every seventy hours then you send it in. I'll give you contact info for the people I see regularly, and if you can't get me on the phone or if they don't know where I am, then it's a safe bet I'm dead," I said.

"But what if you're dead and it wasn't Carmen?"

"I'm a superstitious man, but I don't believe in coincidence," I replied.

"Okay, I'll do whatever you need me to do, Zayvion, you know that."

After writing down the numbers he needed, we shook hands and I left. I felt like all my loose ends were tied up nicely now and I could get back to the business of my business. As soon as I got behind the wheel of my car I got the video from Shmurda, and I took a second to watch it. Other dudes would've felt bad about having someone they once loved brutally sodomized until they were too broken to beg, but not me. In my opinion, Rocko had earned every inch of dick he'd had to take for every second, minute and hour he'd had to take it. The price one paid for disloyalty could never be too high when you were dealing with a real nigga, and your enemy had to be crushed completely, to ensure they never again get the chance to come for you. I didn't watch the entire video because there was literally hours of nothing except Rocko getting fucked. In the end, his ass looked exactly like a baboons, but it was shredded and bleeding like he'd taken a blast from a twenty gauge. When they were done using him for a blow up-doll he was thrown into an oil drum full of rats, the lid was welded on, and he was buried alive. I forwarded the video to Hector with a simple message that said it was done, and then I erased it from my phone. I started my car and pointed it in the direction of my home, enjoying the sights and sounds of the world around me more than I could remember doing in a long time. Being in such a good mood gave me a great idea, so I stopped off at the florist and got three dozen of assorted roses to take home with me. One thing I knew was that women loved to get flowers for no reason. An hour later, I'd arrived at my destination, and I felt like the luckiest mufucka in the world.

"Honey, I'm home!" I yelled, coming through the front door.

"In the kitchen!"

I made my way to the kitchen where I found Abby stuffing her face full of waffles.

"Aww, babe, they're beautiful," Alexis cooed.

"Yeah they are," Burnette chimed in.

"I just felt like you all deserved something almost as beautiful as you," I said, handing each woman a dozen roses.

Alexis was cooking, but she stepped away from the stove to give me a quick kiss. Burnette followed her lead. When it came to Abby's turn, she flushed the way she always does, but she still kissed me passionately.

"So is everything taken care of?" Alexis asked.

If I'd had to decide which female was my main bitch, I'd have to say it was Alexis because we had no secrets, but I cared about all these women on some level, so it only made sense that they co-exist together. Certain things would remain on a need to know basis, and right now, Abby didn't need to know that Rocko was dying painfully slow at this moment.

"Everything is good. What have you ladies been up to?" I asked.

"They're trying to make me fat," Abby said, around a mouth full of food.

"We're trying to make sure her and that baby are healthy," Alexis corrected.

"Plus you could stand to put on a few ounces, just for cushion purposes. I swear, I don't know how you're taking the pounding Zayvion puts down right now," Burnette said.

Of course, Abby blushed while the other two laughed and high-fived.

"Oh, don't worry, she can take the dick," I said, smiling at Abby.

"Speaking of your dick, we've been talking, so take this and have a seat." Alexis said, passing me a plate of food.

I had no idea where this conversation was going, but I took my plate and say down across from Abby. Alexis came and took a seat to my right and Burnette sat across from her on my left.

"So, we were wondering, how much pussy do you need?" Alexis asked.

My first response was to laugh out loud, but I could tell by every woman's expression how serious they were being right now.

"I'm not sure I understand the question," I replied, putting a forkful of eggs into my mouth and chewing slowly.

"Well, basically, we feel like the three of us can satisfy every want and need you could possibly have, especially since we don't have limitations in the bedroom. Therefore, we don't see a reason for you to deal with another female," Burnette said.

"We're not telling you what to do, Zay, but we all like the idea of being a family with you at the center," Abby said.

"Okay," I replied.

"O-okay? That's it, it's that easy?"Alexis asked warily.

"Were you expecting to have to sell me on the idea? Each of you is an amazing woman in her own right, so how could coming together, in every sense of the word, be a bad thing?" I asked, looking around the table.

"I mean, we feel the same way, but we didn't know how you would take such a serious step. Given the fact that you're going through a divorce," Burnette said.

"The only thing I'm going through is realizing I loved some-one for a long time that wasn't worthy of my love," I replied, looking directly at Abby.

"Are we worthy of your love?" Abby asked.

"Absolutely," I replied without hesitation.

"Well, now that the hard part is over, we just have to work on the details," Alexis said.

"Such as?" I asked, going back to eating my food.

"We all want to live together, like a real family, and we want to take the hustle to the next level," Burnette replied.

"Sounds interesting. Weigh it out for me," I said.

"So we figured you might not want any of us working inside the prisons anymore, which means we needed other options. I could go back to working at a hospital, which gives us access to legal drugs," Abby said.

"I could work for the local police department wherever we decide to relocate to," Burnette said.

"And I can apply to work for the FBI," Alexis concluded.

Hearing the last two ideas stopped my fork in mid-air on the way to my mouth, but not because I thought they were crazy, but because I thought they were bold. Putting my fork down, I let what they'd said roll around in my head while I figured out what I wanted to say.

"Why law enforcement?" I asked finally.

"Because knowledge is power, and information is key. Us being on one side of the law can only help you in your business," Alexis replied.

"It's been tried before," I said.

"Not by us though. You actually have women around you that are loyal to *you*, not money or power. That's a rare thing," Burnette said.

"What do you think Abby?" I asked.

"I think that you know we're right, but you're probing to see if we're fully committed. We are. Every woman at this table will drink your cum, your blood, or the kool-aid if it's laced with arsenic. Why? Because even with your flaws, you still managed to give us a love to hold onto, and you gave it to us when we all needed it most. I don't know how it's possible for a man to be going through what you were and still manage to make each of us feel special, but you did and we love you for it. Let us show you that," Abby replied sincerely.

The eloquence with which she spoke blew me away, and fed my ego at the same time. I knew she was right about me wanting to make sure they were committed, but the look on each woman's face said it all.

"Okay, so are we gonna do a group wedding ceremony?" I asked, smiling.

"That's a conversation for after your divorce is final," Alexis replied, giving the other two women a knowing look.

"Oh Lord, what have I done?" I wondered aloud.

"You upgraded," Burnette replied, smiling.

I couldn't argue with that truth.

"So, where did you wanna live?" I asked.

We all kicked around ideas about where the perfect spot to relocate would be. The school system definitely had to be factored in because of Alexis's three kids, plus we needed a lot of room because Abby said she wanted at least two more kids. I'd thought Alexis would flip out at this declaration, but apparently they'd discussed it ahead of time, because there wasn't even a pause in conversation after Abby said it. It was hard for me to believe what was happening right before my very eyes, but it was beautiful to witness. They'd thought I'd saved them by giving them love, but really it was a two-way street. They'd seen me at my lowest and took a chance on a nigga, and that wasn't something they had to do. Just like Carmen they'd had a choice, but they'd chosen to keep it one hundred, and give back the love and loyalty I'd given. I respected that. Once we were finished with the serious conversation, Alexis warmed my food up, and we sat around the table laughing and joking. I was more than content to just chill with my ladies all day, but a text message changed all that.

"I can always tell when you get a message from Carmen. What does she want?" Alexis said.

"To talk, she says," I replied.

"Didn't that involve butt-naked Chinese food delivery last time?" Burnette asked.

"It did," Abby replied.

"Sounds like a bad idea," Alexis said.

I was just about to agree, when Carmen sent me a picture of her divorce papers on the dining room table with a pen next to them.

"Well now, that makes shit interesting," I mumbled.

"What?" Alexis asked.

I passed her my phone, and watched each woman's expression as it made it around the table. Without a word, Alexis got up and went to the bathroom that was just down the hall. She was only in there for a few seconds, and then she was back by my side, putting a blue pill next to my glass of orange juice.

"I don't understand," I said, looking at her with a confused expression.

"Abby, send her a reply that says he'll be there around dinner time," Alexis stated calmly.

"So, you want me to go?" I asked.

"I think you should so you can get this shit done and over with, but if you're going to her house, you're going smelling like my pussy," Alexis replied.

"And mine," Burnette said.

"Mine too," Abby joined in, smiling.

"Hold up. All three of you, at the same time? Are you trying to break my dick?" I asked, looking around the table.

"Aww, baby, it won't break. Besides, we'll be gentle," Alexis said, picking up the little blue pill and feeding it to me.

Once I'd washed it down with my juice, all three women stood up, and I was led upstairs to Alexis's bedroom. I wondered how this was gonna go, but Alexis immediately took charge.

"Alright, we're gonna do this by age. Burnette, you get the dick first and I'll start out riding his face. Abby, you lay down beside him and he's gonna be fucking you with my toy. After an appropriate amount of time we'll switch positions and move in a counter-clockwise motion, which means Abby will get the face next. Once everyone has had dick, toy, and face we'll switch up the line-up and form a train, again going by age. Burnette will get fucked from the back, in her pussy and ass, while she licks my pussy, and I lick Abby's pussy. After everyone has had their backshot, we're gonna see who can make him cum the quickest by sucking his dick. And before you ask, yes, we'll wash it off since its going in our asses first. Now, when the scheduled activities are done, we'll do requests. That little blue pill will work for at least four hours and you already know the type of stamina he has without it, so remember this is a marathon and not a sprint. When this is over, everyone in this room will be sore, but supremely satisfied. Any questions?" Alexis asked, looking around.

No one said anything, but I was actually a little scared.

"Well then, let's get to work. Mr. Miller, would you be so kind as to get naked for us," Alexis requested.

Before I could move, Abby was pulling at my pants and Burnette had my shirt up over my head. They didn't waste any time shedding their clothing either, and I suddenly found myself on my back on Alexis's California king sized bed with Burnette on top of me.

"Here, take this," Alexis said, passing me a dildo.

Abby laid down next to me with her foot near my head and I pushed the toy slowly inside her. Alexis straddled my face, bringing her sweet smelling pussy inches from my lips, while Burnette slipped my dick inside her. I watched as Alexis leaned forward and kissed Burnette softly. And then we all moved together.

Aryanna

Chapter 17

Carmen

I took a deep breath before opening my eyes and pulling the trigger. The feeling of the gun in my hand and the kick from the three-round bursts I was firing was intoxicating, and I fed on that high as I shredded my target. Once I emptied the clip on the AR-15, I put it down and picked up the M-16. With no hesitation, I took careful aim and let that bitch breathe, making confetti out of the target at the far end of the range. I hit the necessary button to bring the clips holding the paper cutout towards me, switched it for a fresh poster and then sent it back down the range. After emptying the clip for the M-16, I put it down and picked up the Tech-9. It wasn't really good for long range, but I loved the way the barrel lit up when I let the bullets fly and the shells rained.

When Zayvion had come to the house and brought me the Glock that ended up deading the side bitch, he'd thought I was living unarmed. If he could see me now, he might have second thoughts about taking my words so lightly. The last time we'd spoken, I'd made him a promise that I would keep because I'd be damned if I let some loose leg bitch have my man! I'd put in too much work, and that meant that nigga owed me a future. He didn't get to rewrite history based on the shit that had happened in the last few months. He didn't get to erase the years where we only had each other and hope. That nigga definitely didn't get to leave me pinching pennies, while he and the next bitch moved on to live their best lives! Just the thought of that made me pop a fresh clip in the Tech-9 and pull the trigger until the shells sounded off like wind chimes in the night. When I'd texted Zay earlier, I knew the thought of me signing the divorce papers would entice him to come over, but that just showed me he thought I was playing with his mufuckin' ass. My rage had been instantaneous, but luckily Karseea had been there so I could escape the house and come to the gun range. Admittedly, I felt a little better, but it was still eating at me that Zayvion thought that he had the moral high ground to treat me this way. The Bible said that a sin was a sin, so how did mine outweigh his? I felt like Zay would see that shit if he just stopped to think, but the nigga stayed with business to handle. Business I was no longer a part of, or reaping the benefits of. I was determined to make him see though, if it was the last thing I did. I reloaded all of the guns and let loose one more time before picking my shit up and heading out. Considering it was still early, I decided to head to the outlet and do a little retail therapy. I might not still have access to Zay's money, but I still had plenty of his credit cards that I could set fire to. One hour and two thousand dollars later, I still wasn't feeling better, so I gave up on the idea of shopping. Before I knew it, I was driving around aimlessly on some nostalgic shit, popping up at places Zay used to take me to on dates, or spots where we used to pull over and fuck. Going back down memory lane I realized Zay wasn't just my nigga, he was *my nigga*. No one else in the world had mattered to me, besides him and my brother, and now I felt completely lost without both. It wasn't just that I didn't know who Mrs. Zayvion Miller was any more, I didn't know who Carmen Vargas was either. A bitch was all the way lost!

I rode around for a little while longer before deciding I had enough. After stopping at a 7-Eleven for a pack of Black & Mild, I rolled through the projects and got me an ounce of weed. Once I found me a nice secluded spot to park, I rolled the tobacco out of one of the Blacks and then I stuffed it with weed. It had been awhile since I'd blown, so I was only a third of the way through the cigar, before my mind opened up like a galaxy in space. Once I got to the halfway point, I had to put that bitch out or I knew I wouldn't be able to find my way back home. I leaned my seat back on some paranoid shit because I didn't want the cops to see me sitting here stuck, and then some wild shit happened. It was like my eyes became a projection screen and I could see my thoughts moving on the roof of my truck. I watched the whole situation with Zayvion unfold, looking at all the ways I went left, when I should've hung a right or busted a U-turn. If I could do it all again, I knew exactly how I'd do it differently, but even in my current state of mind I knew there were no do-overs. The only way to get over this shit was to go through it, but that only worked if Zay went through it with me. I couldn't force him to do that, or could I? The moment I asked myself that question, I felt like that girl in that movie, *Lucy*, when she gets to access one hundred percent of her mind. For the first time, I was seeing clearer than Noah when he built the ark!

With my idea still taking shape in my mind, I put my seat back up, started my truck and headed back to the projects. Once I had what I needed, I went to Burger King and got something to eat. Part of me just had the munchies, but part of me wanted to see if my plan still made sense when I wasn't dancing on clouds. As luck would have it, it did still make sense and with that confirmed, I headed straight home.

"Damn, you smell good," Karseea said, when I came through the door and walked past her.

"Jealous?"

"Hell yeah, and I'm hoping you saved me some," she replied.

"Where are the kids?"

"The babies are sleeping because they just ate a half an hour ago, and the toddlers are in the play room," she replied.

"In the ashtray," I said, tossing her the keys to my truck.

With her momentarily preoccupied, I went straight to the kitchen and started pulling out everything needed for me to cook dinner. I figured steak with loaded baked potatoes, and a vegetable would make a decent enough meal. By the time I had everything out and I was doing my prep, Karseea wandered in looking like a wet cat.

"You gonna make it?" I asked.

"That shit was fire! I only smoked half of what you had left and I'm telling you I'm up there in the nosebleed seats."

"Well, I'm gonna need you to have your feet on the ground before Zayvion gets here," I said.

"You want me to take the kids out again?"

"No, you can just camp out down in the basement with them. Put up the tent for RJ and Ariel, and let them watch whatever movies they want," I replied.

"Mmm, popcorn," she said, dreamily.

"Yeah, your high ass needs to start eating sooner than later, so you can mellow out. You're in a safe place, but you're still gonna be looking after kids."

"I got you," she replied, going to the cabinet and grabbing a box of Thin Mint cookies. Her next stop was the refrigerator, where she pulled out half a gallon of milk, and disappeared into the living room without a glass. All that I could do was shake my head and refocus on the task at hand. Zayvion had said he'd be here by dinnertime, which left me about an hour and a half, but I wasn't expecting him to be on time. While the steaks thawed, I decided to go with creamed corn because I knew that Zay liked that. I made sure the wine was chilling, and then I went to take a quick shower. I came back downstairs smelling like chocolate and cinnamon, but I had on a sweat suit so Zay wouldn't think I was up to some bullshit. By the time I got the steaks in the pan, Karseea was taking shit down to the basement for the kids. Sooner than expected, I heard the front door open and moments later, Zayvion strolled into the kitchen.

"Rough night?" I asked, looking at his disheveled appearance.

"Rough day. What's your excuse?"

"I'm alone in my house, and I ain't trying to impress nobody," I replied honestly.

"So the kids ain't here?"

"Oh no, they're here. Would you like to spend some time with them?" I asked politely.

"If it's not too much trouble," he replied sarcastically.

"No, it's fine, dinner is still cooking. I think you might want to take a shower though, because I can smell you from here."

"Technically, I'm not your man, so I don't have to pass your smell test," he replied.

"You're right, but would you rather I tell you that you smell like rotten ass pussy or your daughter tell you?"

"Hey, Zayvion, I didn't hear you come in. How are-damn! Is that you smelling like that?! Bruh, you need to take that bitch to the clinic ASAP! You probably melted the leather seats in your car, huh?" Karseea asked.

"My point exactly," I said, laughing at the horrified expression on Karseea's face.

Zayvion didn't crack a smile or say shit else, he just turned around and headed upstairs.

"Now that nigga know he foul for coming up in here like that," Karseea said, once he was out of earshot.

"Don't worry about it, everything is gonna work out. Trust me."

"Trust me, give that nigga a shot of penicillin before you do anything with him. And whatever you do, bitch, you better not drink after him!" she said, dead serious.

Despite the situation, I couldn't help laughing, especially with the faces this crazy ass girl was making. I wasn't blind to the fact of what Zayvion was doing though. After all, he did state his intentions the last time that he was here. I just wasn't fazed because I knew my plan would work.

"You got everything set up in the basement?" I asked.

"You ever tried to put up a tent when you're high? All I'm saying is I ain't no dummy, but that tent ain't no bitch either."

"I have faith you'll figure it out, now scoot," I said, motioning her out of the kitchen.

Once she was gone, I added my secret ingredients, herbs, and spices, and then I popped the potatoes in the microwave. Twenty minutes later, I was putting the finishing touches on everything when Zay came into the kitchen with Ariel on his shoulders and RJ clinging to his leg.

"Mommy, we caught Daddy!" Ariel said, excited.

Seeing how happy my daughter was hurt more than smelling another woman on my husband ever could. I had to suppress the rage that was constantly brewing in me because I wanted to lash out and ask Zay how the fuck he couldn't see what this was doing to his daughter. She worshiped her dad, but it was more important to teach me a lesson than work at putting our family back together? Maybe for him it was, but not for me.

"Where did you catch him at sweetie?" I asked.

"He was in the hall outside the playroom, and he tried to run, and we caught him," Ariel replied, smiling proudly.

"And now, I caught you," Karseea said, sneaking up behind them and pulling Ariel off Zay's shoulders.

The squeals and giggles were instant, yet refreshing, because it reminded me of good days and simpler times. I was determined to get back to those days.

"RJ, go with Ariel, Karseea has a surprise for you," I said.

His eyes lit up at the word surprise, but I could clearly see the hesitation to let Zay go. Zayvion must've felt it too, because he scooped RJ up in his arms.

"I'll come see you before I leave, okay?" Zay asked.

"Okay," RJ replied softly.

His sadness was almost unbearable, but when Zay covered his face with kisses, he started laughing and squealing just like his cousin had. Instead of putting him down, Zay carried him down to the basement. I used the moment alone to wipe the tears from my eyes and get my shit together, because crying wasn't gonna win this war. Only ruthless determination would. By the time Zay came back upstairs I'd fixed both of our plates and was carrying them to the dining room.

"Grab the wine," I said.

"Don't be bossing me around."

I didn't say what was on the tip of my tongue, instead I took my seat and waited for him to show up with the wine.

"Thank you," I said, accepting the glass that he poured me.

"Don't mention it."

"They miss you, you know," I said, casually.

"And I miss them, but I'm sure that you already knew that and that's why you had them here."

"They're here because they live here, and tonight won't be about some lame attempt at seduction," I replied.

"Cause you're above that," he said sarcastically.

"Because there's no need."

"Ah, that's right. I believe the last time we shared a meal you told me that we will be together, or you'd kill me," he said, smiling as he took his seat across from me.

My only response was to put my knife to work, cutting my steak and chewing it slowly, while staring him in the eyes.

"You don't scare me, Carmen."

"I almost believed you when you said that," I replied, smiling.

Now it was his turn to stare at me while chewing his food. Unlike last time, the silence wasn't uncomfortable for me, but I could tell that he was still trying to figure out what angle I was playing.

"So, the divorce papers," he said, a few moments later.

"What about them?"

"Don't play games, Carmen."

"Since when did you become so uptight? It must be because you're fucking white girls now," I said playfully.

"I didn't come here to talk about who I'm fucking."

"Really? You really didn't think that would come up in conversation, when you came to my house smelling like a public service announcement for every STD ever?" I asked.

I had to give him points, the nigga knew he had no legs to stand on, and so he shut his mouth for once.

"What do you want to do about custody of Xavier?" I asked finally.

"What do you mean?"

"I mean, I love that little boy and I don't wanna give him up," I replied honestly.

He didn't respond immediately, but I could smell the wood burning as he ate his food. I didn't press the issue. I simply enjoyed my own meal while silently counting in my head.

"You're a good mother, Carmen, and I want that for all my kids, so why don't we do joint custody all the way around."

I lifted my wine glass in salute and he mimicked the gesture.

"Everything else seemed pretty much standard, right?" I asked.

"Y-yeah, it's standard."

"Okay, well I signed the papers and they're in the box with a few of your things sitting on my bed upstairs. Why don't you put everything in your car now so the kids don't have to see that," I suggested.

"Good idea."

When he stood up, he did so on wobbly legs, but he physically shook it off and made his way down the hallway. About a minute and half later, I heard the loud thud of his body hitting the floor upstairs, and that made me smile. I lifted my glass in a salute to his now empty chair.

Chapter 18

Zay

Two days later

It was a fight to open my eyes, and when I managed to achieve my goal, I realized I was having the same dream I always had. At least, I thought it was a dream. People weren't supposed to feel in dreams, but I could feel something holding my wrists and ankles in place. I could feel Carmen's weight on top of me, even though I couldn't understand a word she was saying. So, was I dreaming? The fact that I could now feel her warm pussy throbbing around my dick had me thinking yes and no.

"Car-men," I whispered, trying desperately to fight through the fog and confusion reality was hiding behind.

If this wasn't a dream, then this shouldn't be happening, but there was a voice in my mind telling me how good it felt, and I couldn't argue with that voice. I thought I could feel Carmen's hands on my chest, but everything was in slow motion like we were under water. It had to be a dream. It had to be, because Carmen never rode my dick this slow, and she never cried while we were having sex. Finally understanding that I was dreaming did allow me to enjoy what was happening a little more. I couldn't move my arms or legs, but I could definitely lift with my hips. The first time I did it Carmen almost went flying, and that made me laugh. She was ready the next time though, and when I bucked she rode. Even though I was seeing with double vision, I could tell that her tears had been replaced with a strong determination that made her look like her old self.

"Beautiful," I thought aloud.

When she threw her head back I knew what was happening, and a few seconds later I felt her rain on me. Even in a dream I knew she wouldn't stop. In real life I would've held out and let her cum multiple times, but for some reason, I was too tired for that. And so in the middle of her full gallop, I gave up control and came without warning. I knew she felt my cum, women could always feel it and that's why a man couldn't fake it without a condom on. She kept right on riding though, and I wished her the best as I closed my eyes in search of a new dream. I didn't know how much time had passed, but it felt like time had passed, yet when I opened my eyes again I was having the same dream. The only difference was Carmen wasn't riding me the same way she had been, because instead of looking at her face, I was looking at her nice fat ass. Watching the way she made my dick disappear was hypnotizing. I mean, I could literally see her pussy juices running down my shaft as she bounced on me like a pogo stick! To me that was beyond sexy, but then I witnessed a miracle because when I moved my hips, her pussy juice went from clear to white instantly. Her body started shaking so much that it made mine shake, and without meaning to I came again. This time my eyes closed all by themselves.

"Daddy, wake up. Wake up, Daddy, I made you something."

My eyes felt like sandbags, but I still managed to open them enough to see the brightly colored paperAriel was holding up to my face.

"Thank-you," I stated slowly, hoping I was smiling, because I couldn't tell if my cheeks were moving.

"Get better, Uncle Zay," RJ said, holding up his picture for me to see.

Just past his little head, I could see Carmen standing behind them, and she was smiling at me.

"Zayvion, we love you."

It seemed like her words echoed in my brain endlessly as I lost the fight to keep my eyes open, but I had no doubt I would dream of her again. From what I knew about dreams, they were alleged to be your subconscious working through the problems that your conscious mind couldn't tackle, but all my dreams had the common theme of family. How could they be a problem?

"Wake your ass up, nigga!"

This command was delivered with the force of God, and it was accompanied by a vicious slap that rattled my brain. My eyes flew open and I came face-to-face with Carmen. Not dream Carmen either, ten ways of angry black woman Carmen.

"Bitch, I'll knock you—"

My threat got lost in my throat when I realized that I couldn't use my arms or legs. My mind was clear though, so I knew with certain ink that this wasn't a dream. This was trouble with all capital letters.

"Carmen, why the fuck do you have me tied down to your bed?" I asked, with all the calm I could muster.

"It's our bed, and we can get to that later. Where the fuck is my brother?"

"Huh?" I replied, feigning confusion. This tactic earned me another slap that sent the spit in my mouth flying, and my anger into the kill zone.

"Don't play with me, Zayvion, where is my god damn brother!"

"I don't know, but I know if you hit me one more motherfuckin' time, bitch, I'ma beat your brains loose," I promised.

"How, nigga? You know magic?" she asked, slapping the shit out of me again.

I could taste the blood in my mouth, but I swallowed it along with any smartass retorts. She could have her fun for now, but sooner or later it would be my turn and I would handle her rough.

"It's all over the fucking news that Rocko escaped, but I ain't heard from him and neither has Abby," she said.

"Okay, so why the fuck are you asking me? Obviously, the nigga is on the run, ain't that what you wanted?"

"He wouldn't run without contacting me or Abby, so what did you do, Zayvion?"

"Carmen, he just broke out and you think his first call is gonna be to you? He's not gonna worry about getting out of the country or not getting caught, he's gonna call you?" I asked sarcastically.

"Nigga, it's been two days! He wouldn't go two days without letting me know something so—"

"Wait, hold up! Two days? Carmen, you've had me strapped to this bed for two god damn days?" I asked, feeling the prickling of panic in my mind.

"Yeah, so? I fed you and fucked you, you're fine. Where's my brother?"

"Carmen, if you know what's good for you you'll untie me from this bed now," I said.

"You would be arrogant enough to threaten me when I *know* there's nothing that you can do to me. I'ma need you to stay focused on the topic at hand, and tell me where my brother is."

"For the last time, I don't know where the fuck your brother is. Now untie me," I repeated.

"Tell me what the escape plan was."

"Carmen, I'm not playing with you, your brother—"

Another head turning smack stopped my sentence, but it also made me test the strength of my bindings, because I tried to leap on her mufuckin helmet!

"Now, Zayvion, if I didn't know any better, I'd think that you wanna hit me. Why? Haven't I been good to you? Haven't these past forty-eight hours of good loving I put on you reminded you of what you've been missing?"

"You had to drug me to get me to fuck you, you pathetic bitch," I replied smiling.

"No I didn't have to because you're a pussy hound and you'll fuck anything, but it was more fun for me this way. Big bad Zayvion Miller tied down and made a slave to my pussy. Let's not act like you didn't fuck me back, sweetheart, and since you came without hesitation, I guess that makes you my bitch, huh?"

"I'ma tell you like you told Dara, this ain't gonna end how you think it is. You need to untie me," I said.

"Yeah, yeah, yeah, right, right, right. Tell me the plan to get Rocko out and then we'll see."

I couldn't ever remember being as mad as I was right now. Actually mad wasn't a big enough word, there were literally no words to put what I was feeling into context. I'd always known that Carmen was a brave soul, but this bitch was really trying to dance with the devil in the pale moonlight! For the first time I knew with absolute certainty that blowing this bitch's head off would excite me. I'd have to bide my time though.

"The plan was to have Rocko transported out of prison like he had to go to another county jail for a different case. Once he was out, he was free to do whatever he wanted," I stated.

"So then, where is he? Who picked him up from prison?"

"I told you before I don't know where he is. As for who picked him up, don't ask question that you know I won't answer. Did you try calling his new bitch to see if she'd heard from him?" I asked.

For a minute, Carmen just stared at me with a weird look on her face.

"How did you know he had a new bitch?" she asked slowly.

"Because I keep my ear to the street, what kind of question is that?"

"It's a logical question, especially considering that his new bitch had gone missing too. How do I know that you didn't set it up to look like they ran off together?" She asked.

"Have you been spending your nights watching old gangster movies or something? Bitch, you trippin'! If your brother and his new side bitch is missing, then ding, ding, ding, they're on the run!"

"Maybe. I don't know, and I really don't trust you," she admitted.

"Right, because I'm the one who laces your food, and then ties you down to have sex with you," I replied sarcastically.

"Is that really why you think that I did all of this? No, I did it—"

"Mommy!" Ariel called, banging on the door.

"Come in, baby," Carmen replied.

Seconds later my daughter and nephew came into view, clutching their drawings and further proving that I hadn't been dreaming.

"Daddy we made you more pictures," Ariel said, holding hers up for me to see.

RJ did the same thing.

"Thank you both, I love them," I said, around the lump in my throat.

"You're welcome," they replied in unison.

Once they'd put their new pictures in the stack with the others on my night stand they both kissed me on the cheek before leaving the room.

"That's why I did it," Carmen said softly.

I couldn't say anything, I could only let the tears leak from my eyes onto my pillow.

"We're a family Zayvion, and not one that happened by accident. You and I planned a life together with a lifetime of memories to be made, and I know that I did my part in fucking that up, but I also know that we can get back what we had. All we have to do is try."

"Is this what trying looks like Carmen?" I asked, pulling on my restraints for emphasis.

"Yes, because I knew that all you needed was to be at home with your family, and not out in the streets letting bitches fall on your dick. You just needed time to remember what was actually real in your life, and who really loved you. We love you, Zayvion. I love you," she progressed, leaning over and kissing my lips softly.

She didn't try to force her tongue in my mouth, but instead alternated between brief kisses and sucking on my lips. After a few moments, I felt her reach under the blanket she'd cover me with to see if she was turning me on, and after feeling my dick, she backed away from me completely. I watched as she let her robe drop to the floor, and then she snatched the blanket off before crawling in between my legs.

"Carmen, untie me," I said.

"Not yet, baby."

Before I could say anything else, she had half my dick down her throat and her hand was massaging my balls rhythmically. It didn't matter how many times I'd seen this show over the years, it never got old.

166

"Carmen," I moaned.

She didn't say anything. She just kept taking more of me in her mouth until I could feel the heat of her breath through her nostrils on my pubic hair. I'd had good head and good pussy from plenty of women, but there was always something different about Carmen, because no one knew me like she did. Her technique had my back off the bed like I was attempting to levitate, and I wasn't ashamed of it. I watched her watching me, knowing that she was the black widow and I was dinner. In her eyes, I saw the shared history that she'd spoken on before, and as crazy as this situation was, I understood why she'd done it this way.

"C-Carmen wait, baby, we need to talk," I said, when she'd finally released me from in between her jaws.

"We can talk later," she replied, crawling up my body until she'd once again straddled me.

"Baby just wait, I-I."

It was no use because I was inside her again, and she was moving with a purpose.

"Carmen, the police are here," Karseea said, bursting into the room.

Nothing else might've got her off me, but that statement made her move like the house was on fire.

"The cops, what do they want?" she asked, panicked.

"I don't know, they knocked on the door and I used the intercom to tell them I'd be right there," Karseea replied.

"Carmen, untie me," I said.

She completely ignored me, picking up her robe and putting it back on before rushing into our bedroom closet.

"Karseea, untie," I said softly.

"Huh?"

"You heard me, just—"

I shut my mouth as soon as Carmen came back into the room because she was coming at me fast. Before I knew what was happening, she had a ball gag over my head and in my mouth.

"Stay with him," she said to Karseea and then she disappeared out the door.

Karseea closed the door behind her and then went straight to the intercom panel on the wall behind the door. I wanted to make a bunch of noise, but I also wanted to hear what was being said, so I fumed in silence.

"Mrs. Carmen Miller?"

"Yes, that's me," I heard Carmen reply.

"We're looking for your brother, Raynard Vargas, and we have a warrant to search this premises."

That was all Karseea needed to hear to have the *oh fuck* look etched onto her face, and she quickly checked the intercom off.

"Oh, this is bad, this is really bad! They're gonna see you and think I was a part of Carmen's plan, and I can't go down for this shit, Zay. I can't!" she insisted, pacing back and forth at a high rate of speed.

Suddenly she stopped next to me and looked at my dick. She looked at me, looked at my dick again, and then looked back at me.

"Zay, I promise if you go along with this so I don't get in trouble, I'll get you out of this mess. I swear," she said, kicking off her shoes, and then the rest of her clothes.

I didn't have a chance to agree or disagree before she was on the bed next to me.

"Why couldn't you have like an average six inches to work with," she mumbled, throwing a leg over my body so that she could straddle me.

Any other time, the fear I saw on her face would've been comical, but now wasn't the time for laughs. She took a deep breath and then put her hands on my chest to brace herself. In the twenty seconds that this plan had come together, it hadn't crossed my mind what Karseea's pussy would feel like, so the fact that she was tropical storm wet and vise grip tight forced me to stop breathing. The way she moved on me was methodical because she'd take a little dick, then lift completely off, and then she'd take a little more and lift completely off. I had to let her do it her way though, and pray that I didn't cum.

"O-okay, I think I'm ready," she said, looking me in the eyes.

I nodded my head and she began to slowly ride me. Every time she lifted all the way up there was a wet smacking sound that echoed off the walls, and it was turning me on even more.

"I-I've never been so-so wet," she said, clearly mesmerized by her body's response.

The fact that she was moving faster spoke to her comfort level, but the sound of a police radio froze her in mid-stride. The look on her face wasn't fear, it was straight terror. I tried to tell her to keep going, but it came out as nothing more than a mumble. That only left one option. I moved my hips gently the first time and it startled her, but didn't entice her to move. After that, I threw caution to the wind and tried to put her head on the ceiling with each thrust.

"Zay! Zay, wait! Zay, oh shit," she stammered.

I didn't expect her to cum but she did, and that's all it took to crack her code.

Aryanna

Chapter 19

Carmen

"Honestly officers, I don't know where my brother is, but I promise you he's not here. I have four small children in the house, so I definitely wouldn't have a fugitive here, even if he was my brother."

"We understand ma'am, but we still have to do our job. Is there anyone else in the house besides the four children you just mentioned?" the cop asked.

We'd just reached the top of the stairs, and I was hearing something that sounded impossible to me.

"Mrs. Miller, any other occupants?" he asked again.

My only response was to open my bedroom door.

"Oh, oh, my g-God!" Karseea cried.

I could tell by the large amount of cum cascading down Zayvion's dick and balls that this bitch wasn't play acting, and it took everything in me not to snatch her bald on the spot!

"Ex-excuse me, ma'am, if you could just hold on for a second so we can make sure that's not the man we're looking for," the cop said, walking into my bedroom.

His partner stayed in the hallway with me. The truly amazing part was that this bitch didn't stop, she only slowed down! I could tell by the way her body was quivering that she was still deep in the throes of orgasmic shock, and her body literally couldn't let the dick go, but I was still seeing red. After the cop looked Zay in the face, checked under the bed, and in the closet, he came back into the hallway. I was just about to threaten Karseea with imminent death, but the cop was polite enough to close my bedroom door on his way out and insist that we continue on with the search. Even as I walked them from room to room, my mind stayed trapped upstairs, wondering what the fuck they were up there doing at this minute. At one point I was positive I heard a scream, but the lack of reaction from the cops had me questioning myself. Finally, after an agonizing twenty minutes the cops left, and before the front door closed I was already taking the stairs two at a time. I busted into my bedroom expecting to find some variation of what I'd been forced to witness earlier, but it was like nothing had ever happened. Karseea was standing by the window fully dressed, and Zay was tied to the bed with a ball bag in his mouth and a blanket covering him.

"What the fuck was that?" I growled, advancing on Karseea like a hungry lioness.

When she turned toward me and I saw the tears running freely from her eyes, I pulled up short.

"That was me saving your ass from the awkward question of why you have a semi-conscious man tied up. That was me not becoming an accessory to whatever bullshit this is! And that was me compromising my morals by fucking another man, when I'm in a committed relationship. That's what the fuck that was, and you're welcome," she replied, pushing past me and walking out of the room.

In my mind, I'd seen that conversation going a couple different ways, but me feeling like shit wasn't one of those ways. After closing the door, I went to Zayvion and pulled the ball gag off him.

"I bet you enjoyed that," I said.

"Not as much as I would've before."

"Before what?" I asked, sitting in the bed beside him.

"Before I understood your motivation. I mean, I understand you want your family back, but do you realistically think that's possible?"

"Anything is possible, Zayvion, as long as we're willing to put the necessary work in. Happily ever after don't come easy."

"And sometimes they just don't come at all sweetheart," he replied softly.

"Yeah, well now isn't one of those times," I said, standing up and pulling the blanket off of him.

It had been my intention to give him a thorough cleaning, but I could look at him and tell that it was unnecessary.

"Karseea did that so you wouldn't have to deal with it. None of this was easy for her, Carmen, but she put herself on the line. You can't keep forcing her into situations without her onset, that ain't cool."

"The last thing I need or want is a lecture from you," I replied, tossing the blanket back over him, and grabbing the syringe full of special K out of the bedside drawer.

"What the hell are you pumping me full of?"

"Don't worry, it won't kill you," I said, jabbing the needle into his arm and emptying the contents.

It only took a few moments for his eyes to close, but it took a little longer for me to work up the nerve to go find Karseea. Unexpectedly, I found her in the kitchen nursing a glass of Henny.

"You're too light in the ass to pick a fight with some Hennessy," I warned.

"Seemed about as good an idea as picking a fight with you."

"We don't need to fight. I'm sorry for how I reacted, and I'm sorry about putting you in that situation. It's just I wasn't expecting to open the door and see that," I said, taking a seat across from her.

"I definitely hadn't planned on doing that, I mean, I was terrified! And then my body, it just, I can't explain what happened."

"I know what happened, and I'm not blaming you. I did warn you though," I said, chuckling.

Her response was to empty the contents of her glass down her throat quickly.

"We're sooo not having that conversation," she replied, standing and going to pour herself a refill.

"Just remember there's nothing to be gained by telling your boyfriend. You need to take that secret to the grave."

"Sage advice," she said, tossing her shot back.

"I'm gonna give you some more good advice, get out of here. Go have some fun and I don't wanna see you again before ten a.m. tomorrow morning."

"No, Carmen, you've got too much going on for me to leave you right now and—"

"And it's my problem, now go," I said, dismissing further argument.

She put her glass down, gave me a quick hug, and left. I hadn't truly wanted her to leave because I didn't want to be alone, but what Zay had said to me upstairs was true. Karseea had given me sound advice on fighting for my marriage, but she hadn't asked to be my co-defendant. I fixed myself a shot of Henny and made it disappear before I went about the business of making dinner. Based on the dosage I'd given Zay, I knew he wouldn't be eating with us tonight, so I decided to order pizza for me and the kids. I was in the middle of making bottles for the babies when my phone started ringing. When I grabbed it off the table, I was surprised to see that is was Zay's lawyer calling.

"Charles, to what do I owe the pleasure?"

"I'm sorry to bother you, Carmen, but have you seen Zayvion today?" he asked.

"I can't say that I have, Charles, why, is something wrong?"

"No, I just needed his signature on something," he replied nonchalantly.

"Well, since we've decided to put the divorce on hold, I can just come to your office after my errands in the morning and sign whatever you need."

"Y-you're putting the divorce on hold?" he asked.

"Don't seem so shocked, Charles."

"Oh, I'm not. I just wanted to make sure I heard you, so I could say I told you so. I always knew you two would work it out," he said.

"And, you were right. So, I'll see you in the morning?"

"I'll be waiting," he replied, beforehanging up.

I couldn't stop from smiling, even though Zay hadn't exactly agreed to what I wanted. I knew he'd come around though. I was just about to put my phone down when it started ringing again.

"Hotline?" I answered, without bothering to see who it was.

"Carmen, where's Zayvion?"

"A-Abby, is that you?" I asked/

"Yes it's me. Where's Zayvion?

"Uh, Abby? Sweetheart, you can call me and ask about Rocko, but you can't call and ask about my husband," I replied calmly.

"Your *ex*-husband."

"I'm sorry, what did you say?" I asked, certain I hadn't heard her right.

"I said, he's your soon-to-be ex-husband. He doesn't love you, you delusional bitch!"

"Oh, Abigail, I thought that you were so much smarter than what you're demonstrating right now. Let me guess, you fell on his dick and then fell for all his lies," I replied.

"He never had to lie to me, he showed me what was real. And yes, I did fall on his dick, I prayed to it like it was the sweet baby Jesus of Nazareth. My pussy was on him when he came to sign those divorce papers, now where the fuck is he?"

I never would've predicted this little white girl would be so bold, but apparently Zay brought out the animal in everyone.

"Well, if you must know, he's upstairs sleeping in our bed, and his dick smells like my pussy. Have a good evening," I said, hanging up before she could get a word out.

It would be a lie for me to say that Zayvion fucking that bitch didn't piss me off, but I recognized it for the tactic it was. If Rocko found out, it would hurt him deeply. That meant that after that trifling bitch gave birth to my niece, I was gonna erase her from the earth, and smile while doing it. With that business settled, I got back to focusing on the important things, namely the kids. The pizza arrived ten minutes later, and we threw a pizza party, complete with movies and soda. It took me til midnight to get them to bed, but it was worth it to see the tired smiles on their faces. Unfortunately, I still wasn't over Abby's revelations, so I slept on the couch instead of crawling into my bed as originally planned. Despite how comfortable my couch was, I still woke up with a stiff neck, and the smell of coffee filling my nostrils.

"I thought I said I didn't wanna see you before ten," I said, walking into my kitchen to find Karseea sitting at the table with a mug in her hand.

"I'm only a couple hours early, and besides this house looks like a tornado hit it, so I know them kids gave you a run for your money."

"Girl! I love them, but you damn right they did," I replied, fixing myself a cup of coffee.

"Well, they're still sleep, and I just propped the little ones up with bottles in their cribs. I was gonna check on Zay for you, but I noticed you added a padlock to the outside of your door."

"Yeah, I didn't want the kids constantly running in there when I'm not upstairs," I said.

"And, you don't want him to get out either. Carmen, are you sure you're going about this the best way?" she asked, gently.

"You were the one who told me to fight for my marriage, and that I didn't have to fight fair."

"I also said you didn't have to go to an extreme. I mean, if Zayvion loves you then let him love you," she stated.

"What do you mean if? I know he loves me, Karseea, because we were already making progress before the cops showed up. I wasn't fucking Zay, we were finally back to making love."

"Okay, so why not untie him?" she asked logically.

"Because he still needs more time to see that this is where he needs to be. It's not about sex or his ability to be faithful, it's about our family coming before everything else." I replied passionately.

Given that Karseea didn't have the time and experience invested into her relationship that I had in mine, I didn't know if she could understand where I was coming from. I knew I was doing the right thing though.

"I saw on the news this morning that they found an abandoned car owned by a nurse that worked at the same prison your brother escaped from. They found it about a mile from a boss station, and now they're speculating that the two of them are together," she said.

"I hope so. I hope he made a clean getaway because that means everything is gonna work out after all," I replied smiling.

"Alright, so I know you have stuff to do today, so why don't you go take a shower and check on your husband while I get breakfast started?"

"Sounds like a plan," I replied, taking my cup of coffee and heading upstairs.

I looked in on the kids first, before pulling the key out of my bra and unlocking the door to my room. As expected, Zayvion was still knocked out, and once I made sure that he was breathing, I hopped in the shower. Ten minutes later, I was smelling good, feeling better, and looking forward to the day ahead. The weather looked nice out my window, so I put on a tank top and some hip hugging capris before stepping into my Air Force Ones.

"Car-Carmen, untie me," Zayvion slurred.

At first, I thought he was talking in his sleep, but then I saw that his eyes were barely open and tracking my movements.

"Just rest, Zay, we'll talk when I get back."

"Carmen, the-the police are c-coming. Untie me," he insisted, sounding like an alcoholic in the middle of a wild bender.

"The cops have already been here, bae. Just go back to sleep," I replied, grabbing my purse on my way out the door.

I made sure to secure the lock before making my way back to the kitchen.

"Mmm, smells good in here," I said.

"You know I got those cooking skills from my momma."

"Well just make sure that you feed my babies, and that includes my husband, who is now awake," I said, passing her the key to my room.

"I got you. How long are you gonna be gone?"

"No more than a couple hours. You can let the kids see Zayvion, but only when you're in the room. And whatever you do, don't ride my husband's dick again," I replied, smiling sweetly despite the seriousness of my tone.

"Trust me. I don't want no more of that."

"Good talk. I'll see you later," I said, turning and heading outside to my truck.

Seeing Zay's Cadillac parked next to me reminded me that I needed to move it, but that could wait until I got back from running around. I got in my truck and left, but about a block from the house I realized that the odor of weed was real strong in my nose. That's when I realized that not only did I have weed still in the trucks but my guns too, and I made a quick U-turn. After grabbing the weed out of the center console, the Glock .40 from under my driver's seat, and the bag full of guns out of the back, I ran back into the house. It had been my intention to dump everything in my hall closet and deal with it later, but as soon as I opened the front door that all changed.

"Bitch what the fuck are you going?" I asked, spotting Zayvion with his arm around Karseea at the bottom of the stairs.

"I, I'm just trying to help him. Carmen, he-he needs help," she stammered nervously.

"Help? He needs help with what? Leaving? You trying to help my husband leave me?" I asked, shutting the door behind me and dropping everything on the floor.

Everything except the Glock .40.

"Carmen, you're not thinking straight because if you were, you'd know that this ain't the way to do things," Karseea replied.

"Bitch, who are you to tell me how to do things, you're just the latest hoe to get fucked," I said angrily.

"I didn't ask to get fucked. I was trying to help your crazy ass!" she yelled.

"Right, and that's why you had to cum on the dick, huh? You couldn't have helped me no other way except to spread your legs and be a cum dumpster? You know what I think? I think you're trying to sneak Zay out of here in the hopes that he'll make you one of his groupies. It's a damn shame you're that thirsty." I said, shaking my head in disgust.

"Thirsty? Bitch, you're the one who can't get over the nigga and move on with your life! You're obsessed! I tried to help you, but it's clear that the nigga just don't want you, so let him go!"

"So a hoe like you can have him? Bitch please, miss me with that Mickey Mouse psychobabble bullshit and step the fuck away from my man," I demanded.

"Carmen, he's not your man! My God, do you even hear yourself anymore? I don't want him, but he damn sure don't want your looney   ass."

"Yeah, that's what a hoe would say. You're free to leave now," I replied, stepping out of the way of the door. She helped Zayvion to the couch before heading towards the door.

"You're a fucked-up person, Carmen," she said, turning to face me.

"Like your opinion matters. Just make sure you get a Plan B, bitch, because I ain't raising no more illegitimate kids."

For some reason what I'd said made her smile.

"Nah, I don't think I'll do that. I wouldn't mind having a baby by Zayvion. Because I'm smart enough to know that if I treat him right he'll bless me with that good dick whenever I need it. Oh, and just to be clear, we kept fucking after you left with the cops. I came three times on that big black dick, and then I sucked him until—"

She didn't get to finish her sentence before the two shots I fired pushed her teeth through her brain.

"Carmen, stop. It's over, and you have to l-let me go," Zayvion weakly.

"Let you go? After all I've done for you? I don't think so, now get your ass back upstairs and get them clothes off," I ordered, leveling my pistol at him.

He was slow to stand, but eventually he made it to his feet. Before he could take a step though, the sound of approaching police sirens filled the air.

"I told you to let-let me go," he said, shaking his head sadly.

"Y-you called the cops on me?" I asked in disbelief.

"No, I had a plan in place. If I suddenly went missing, the video of you killing Iesha would go public."

"Video? There's no video, because I didn't kill Iesha," I replied smiling.

"When you fucked her with my pistol, you made her say that I didn't love her over and over again."

Instantly my smile faltered. There was no way for him to know that unless he was there, and we both know that he wasn't there.

"Mommy what happened to Seea?" Ariel asked from the top of the stairs.

"Everything I've done is because I love you, Zayvion, I love you so much. I know now that you don't love me though, and maybe you never did," I said, shaking my head sadly as tears poured from my eyes.

"I did love you, Carmen. I truly did," he replied.

"Mommy, is Seea hurt?" Ariel asked.

"Carmen Miller, this is the police, come out with your hands up," commanded a voice outside my front door.

"You loved me, Zayvion?" I asked softly.

"Yes, and a part of me always will," he replied genuinely.

"Good. Explain this to the kids when the time comes," I said, putting the gun to my head.

He reacted quickly, but not quick enough. I still pulled the trigger.

Chapter 20

Zay

The immense pain in her eyes had been easy to see, even with my system being full of drugs. I hadn't seen the defeat in her eyes until she raised the gun and put it to her temple.

"Carmen, no!" I screamed, lunging towards her.

I heard the pop from the pistol, and I was by her side fast enough to watch her body before she hit the floor.

"Oh, no, no, no! Come on Carmen, don't do this," I pleaded in fear and desperation.

All I wanted in this moment was for her to open her eyes and smile at me one more time, but I knew she wouldn't.

"Daddy, is Mommy hurt?" Ariel asked.

"Come on, Carmen, come on baby don't leave me," I begged.

The sudden sound of wood splintering as the front door came off its hinges startled me, and my first reaction was to grab Carmen's gun. I never got my hand around the rubber grip before I heard a series of shots and I felt myself lifted off my feet by bullets. I could hear voices telling me not to move. I could hear my kids crying. I could hear my heart beating. And then I couldn't hear anything.

Aryanna

Chapter 21

Seven months later

The view in front of me was one I'd seen before on numerous occasions, but it still wasn't one I enjoyed. Even though the voices of people talking all around me could be heard, I was really hearing God's laughter over the plans I'd made. Once think I'd learned was that no matter how good a plan you had, or what contingencies you made to assist your plan, God would do what he wanted to do. True enough, we had free will, but that really equated to was picking which car to drive on the road of life, not picking the destination. I guess that's why we had to live with regrets because sometimes you thought you were buying a Ferrari, but you ended up with a lemon. Today was my first day of making lemonade. I didn't have a plan per say, I only had a goal, and that was to be better than I was for those that needed me. I know that sounded easy enough, but nothing in life was ever really easy. Not love, marriage, family, or the hustle. You had to claw and scratch for everything you wanted, and then you had to bring willing to kill to keep it. Sometimes that meant the person closest to you had to die. Sometimes that meant you had to die in order to be reborn. Either way, there would be blood.

"All rise! The Honorable Judge Valerie Malley presiding," the bailiff bellowed.

"Be seated," the judge said, taking her seat on the bench.

"Let's see what we have today...the state of Virginia versus Miller. Who here is representing the defense?" the judge asked.

"Charles Swedish, your honor."

"Ah, Mr. Swedish, it seems like we've been here before. Although these circumstances are more bizarre," Judge Malley commented.

"They most certainly are, Your Honor, and that's why we've amended our plea and requested a jury trial," Charles replied.

"Will the defendant please rise," Judge Malley asked.

I took my time standing, but I knew the judge would understand.

"Zayvion Miller...that was your husband?" Judge Malley asked.

"Yes, Your Honor, my late husband, and the father to my unborn child," I replied, rubbing my stomach.

"I'm sorry for your loss. What would you like to change your plea to?" Judge Malley asked.

"Not guilty by reason of insanity..."

The End
(Epic!)

Submission Guideline

Submit the first three chapters of your completed manuscript to ldpsubmissions@gmail.com, subject line: Your book's title. The manuscript must be in a .doc file and sent as an attachment. Document should be in Times New Roman, double spaced and in size 12 font. Also, provide your synopsis and full contact information. If sending multiple submissions, they must each be in a separate email.

Have a story but no way to send it electronically? You can still submit to LDP/Ca$h Presents. Send in the first three chapters, written or typed, of your completed manuscript to:

LDP: Submissions Dept
Po Box 870494
Mesquite, Tx 75187

DO NOT send original manuscript. Must be a duplicate.

Provide your synopsis and a cover letter containing your full contact information.

Thanks for considering LDP and Ca$h Presents.

<u>Coming Soon from Lock Down Publications/Ca$h Presents</u>

BOW DOWN TO MY GANGSTA
By **Ca$h**
TORN BETWEEN TWO
By **Coffee**
BLOOD STAINS OF A SHOTTA **III**
By **Jamaica**
STEADY MOBBIN **III**
By **Marcellus Allen**
BLOOD OF A BOSS **V**
By **Askari**
LOYAL TO THE GAME **IV**
LIFE OF SIN II
By **T.J. & Jelissa**
A DOPEBOY'S PRAYER **II**
By **Eddie "Wolf" Lee**
IF LOVING YOU IS WRONG… **III**
LOVE ME EVEN WHEN IT HURTS **II**
By **Jelissa**
TRUE SAVAGE **VII**
By **Chris Green**
BLAST FOR ME **III**
A BRONX TALE III
DUFFLE BAG CARTEL
By **Ghost**
ADDICTIED TO THE DRAMA **III**
By **Jamila Mathis**
LIPSTICK KILLAH **III**
Mimi

WHAT BAD BITCHES DO **III**

KILL ZONE **II**

By **Aryanna**

THE COST OF LOYALTY **II**

By **Kweli**

SHE FELL IN LOVE WITH A REAL ONE **II**

By **Tamara Butler**

RENEGADE BOYS **III**

By **Meesha**

CORRUPTED BY A GANGSTA **IV**

By **Destiny Skai**

A GANGSTER'S CODE **III**

By **J-Blunt**

KING OF NEW YORK IV

RISE TO POWER II

By **T.J. Edwards**

GORILLAS IN THE BAY II

De'Kari

THE STREETS ARE CALLING II

Duquie Wilson

KINGPIN KILLAZ III

Hood Rich

STEADY MOBBIN' **III**

Marcellus Allen

SINS OF A HUSTLA II

ASAD

TRIGGADALE II

Elijah R. Freeman

MARRIED TO A BOSS 2…

By Destiny Skai & Chris Green

Aryanna

KINGS OF THE GAME II
Playa Ray

IF LOVING HIM IS WRONG…I & II

LOVE ME EVEN WHEN IT HURTS

By **Jelissa**

WHEN THE STREETS CLAP BACK I & II III

By **Jibril Williams**

A DISTINGUISHED THUG STOLE MY HEART I II & III

LOVE SHOULDN'T HURT I II III

RENEGADE BOYS I & II

By **Meesha**

A GANGSTER'S CODE I & II

By J-Blunt

PUSH IT TO THE LIMIT

By **Bre' Hayes**

BLOOD OF A BOSS **I, II, III & IV**

By **Askari**

THE STREETS BLEED MURDER **I, II & III**

THE HEART OF A GANGSTA I II& III

By **Jerry Jackson**

CUM FOR ME

CUM FOR ME 2

CUM FOR ME 3

CUM FOR ME 4

An **LDP Erotica Collaboration**

BRIDE OF A HUSTLA **I II & II**

THE FETTI GIRLS **I, II& III**

CORRUPTED BY A GANGSTA I, II & III

By **Destiny Skai**

WHEN A GOOD GIRL GOES BAD

By **Adrienne**

A GANGSTER'S REVENGE **I II III & IV**

THE BOSS MAN'S DAUGHTERS

THE BOSS MAN'S DAUGHTERS II

THE BOSSMAN'S DAUGHTERS III

THE BOSSMAN'S DAUGHTERS IV

THE BOSS MAN'S DAUGHTERS **V**

A SAVAGE LOVE **I & II**

BAE BELONGS TO ME

A HUSTLER'S DECEIT I, II, III

WHAT BAD BITCHES DO I, II

By **Aryanna**

A KINGPIN'S AMBITON

A KINGPIN'S AMBITION **II**

I MURDER FOR THE DOUGH

By **Ambitious**

TRUE SAVAGE

TRUE SAVAGE II

TRUE SAVAGE **III**

TRUE SAVAGE **IV**

TRUE SAVAGE **V**

TRUE SAVAGE **VI**

By **Chris Green**

A DOPEBOY'S PRAYER

By **Eddie "Wolf" Lee**

THE KING CARTEL **I, II & III**

By **Frank Gresham**

THESE NIGGAS AIN'T LOYAL **I, II & III**

By **Nikki Tee**

GANGSTA SHYT **I II &III**

By **CATO**

THE ULTIMATE BETRAYAL

By **Phoenix**

BOSS'N UP **I , II & III**

By **Royal Nicole**

I LOVE YOU TO DEATH

By Destiny J

I RIDE FOR MY HITTA

I STILL RIDE FOR MY HITTA

By **Misty Holt**

LOVE & CHASIN' PAPER

By **Qay Crockett**

TO DIE IN VAIN

SINS OF A HUSTLA

By **ASAD**

BROOKLYN HUSTLAZ

By **Boogsy Morina**

BROOKLYN ON LOCK I & II

By **Sonovia**

GANGSTA CITY

By **Teddy Duke**

A DRUG KING AND HIS DIAMOND I & II III

A DOPEMAN'S RICHES

HER MAN, MINE'S TOO I, II

CASH MONEY HO'S

By Nicole Goosby

TRAPHOUSE KING **I II & III**

KINGPIN KILLAZ

By **Hood Rich**

LIPSTICK KILLAH **I, II**

CRIME OF PASSION I & II

By **Mimi**

STEADY MOBBN' **I, II**

By **Marcellus Allen**

WHO SHOT YA **I, II**

Renta

GORILLAZ IN THE BAY

DE'KARI

TRIGGADALE

Elijah R. Freeman

GOD BLESS THE TRAPPERS I, II, III

THESE SCANDALOUS STREETS I, II, III

FEAR MY GANGSTA I, II, III

THESE STREETS DON'T LOVE NOBODY I, II

BURY ME A G I, II, III, IV, V

Tranay Adams

THE STREETS ARE CALLING

Duquie Wilson

MARRIED TO A BOSS…

By Destiny Skai & Chris Green

KINGS OF THE GAME II

Playa Ray

BOOKS BY LDP'S CEO, CA$H

TRUST IN NO MAN

TRUST IN NO MAN 2

TRUST IN NO MAN 3

BONDED BY BLOOD

SHORTY GOT A THUG

THUGS CRY

THUGS CRY 2

THUGS CRY 3

TRUST NO BITCH

TRUST NO BITCH 2

TRUST NO BITCH 3

TIL MY CASKET DROPS

RESTRAINING ORDER

RESTRAINING ORDER 2

IN LOVE WITH A CONVICT

Coming Soon

BONDED BY BLOOD 2

BOW DOWN TO MY GANGSTA

Aryanna

CPSIA information can be obtained
at www.ICGtesting.com
Printed in the USA
LVHW020752180820
663382LV00003B/218

9 781949 138795